SILENT BITE

Also by DAVID ROSENFELT

SILENT BITE

David Rosenfelt

MINOTAUR BOOKS
NEW YORK

First published in the United States by Minotaur Books, an imprint of St. Martin's Publishing Group

SILENT BITE. Copyright © 2020 by Tara Productions, Inc. All rights reserved. Printed in the United States of America. For information, address St. Martin's Publishing Group, 120 Broadway, New York, NY 10271.

www.minotaurbooks.com

Library of Congress Cataloging-in-Publication Data

Names: Rosenfelt, David, author.
Title: Silent bite / David Rosenfelt.
Description: First edition. | New York : Minotaur Books, 2020. | Series: An Andy Carpenter novel ; 22
Identifiers: LCCN 2020031595 | ISBN 9781250257147 (hardcover) | ISBN 9781250257154 (ebook)
Subjects: LCSH: Carpenter, Andy (Fictitious character)— Fiction. | GSAFD: Mystery fiction.
Classification: LCC PS3618.O838 S55 2020 | DDC 813/.6—dc23
LC record available at https://lccn.loc.gov/2020031595

Our books may be purchased in bulk for promotional, educational, or business use. Please contact your local bookseller or the Macmillan Corporate and Premium Sales Department at 800-221-7945, extension 5442, or by email at MacmillanSpecialMarkets@macmillan.com.

First Edition: 2020

10 9 8 7 6 5 4 3 2 1

SILENT BITE

This is Terry Banner asking you to remember that you heard it here first."

The red light went off, telling Banner with certainty that he was no longer on the air. He took out his earpiece, removed his microphone, opened his shirt collar, and removed his tie. He hated ties; if the inventor of the tie were still alive, Banner would wish him a miserable death. Strangulation would represent a delicious irony.

"Way to go, Terry. You really nailed it tonight."

Banner accepted the compliment from the cameraman with a nod and a brief "Thanks." The truth was that he had no idea if he had nailed it or not; the cameraman said some version of the same thing after every broadcast. The other truth was that by a half hour after the time he would get to the bar, he'd forget what it was that he had talked about.

Banner was the opinion reporter for a local Scranton, Pennsylvania, station, and each night's opinion was basically a recitation of some series of events that he claimed should leave viewers feeling outraged. Since people never tired of feeling outraged, Banner was the closest thing Scranton had to a media star.

Banner's career had already taken an unusual path. He started out at a small Toledo station, then got noticed by a New York news executive visiting his grandmother in a Toledo suburb. The next thing he knew he was working for Channel 5 in New York.

That's where he started his daily outrages spiel, and he thought he was doing pretty well. Then one day the target of his outrage was the local teachers' union, which turned out to be an unfortunate choice, since the incoming head of the news division turned out to have a sister who was the president of that same union. Banner was gone soon after.

Actually, Banner didn't realize that his ill-fated choice of targets was only a secondary reason for his firing. What was really going on was that the station had information that Banner was involved in unsavory and possibly illegal activities in his life away from the studio. The station preferred to keep that quiet and let people assume that it was the station manager's anger and defense of his sister that led to Banner's termination.

The next thing Banner knew he was back in Scranton. And even though no one would ever accuse him of being an upbeat person, he soon learned that exile wasn't so bad. He became a Scranton celebrity and found out that he liked being the big fish in the small pond.

He brought his outrage shtick with him, and people all over the Scranton area were soon tuning in to find out what they should be pissed off about. So even though when he first left New York he was determined to get back, pretty soon he wasn't thinking about that at all. The cost of living was much less, the women were just as nice and liked him far more than New York women did, and the alcohol went down just the same.

There was another aspect of life in Scranton that represented a pleasant surprise for Banner. In the New York area, he had developed a lucrative sideline of selling opioids. A contact had been easy to make, and quite a few people, including some colleagues, were eager buyers.

It didn't take long to set up a similar operation in Scranton; he didn't even have to change suppliers. He believed he was smart enough to stay under any law enforcement radar, and if the police had noticed him, they hadn't come forward. Before long Banner's unofficial career was earning him more than his on-air work.

On that particular night Banner went to his favorite bar, Shanahan's, in downtown Scranton. For weeks he'd sat in the same seat at the right end of the bar, but then started to feel like Norm from *Cheers,* so he moved to a small table in the far corner. More than occasionally Banner wound up leaving with a female patron, but no such luck on that night.

He arrived at seven o'clock and left at nine forty-five. Towns in this part of Pennsylvania generally closed up early, at least by New York standards, and Scranton was no exception. His blood alcohol level was certainly over the legal limit, and there was never a time that he wouldn't have at least traces of drugs in his body, but he never worried about that. He was conscious of his impairment and drove carefully, and it's not like there was ever traffic at that hour.

Banner's drive home was without incident, and twenty minutes after he left the bar he pulled into his garage. Eighteen seconds after that the .38-caliber bullet entered the back of his head, killing him instantly.

My first cruise is almost over.

Truth be told, I didn't want to do this. I was more than willing to go through life cruise-less. But Laurie and Ricky wanted to go on one, so as we often do, we had a family vote. It would not have taken Gallup to predict that the final tabulation would be two votes in favor of going, and one opposed. I asked for the jury to be polled, but that didn't change the final count.

We boarded one week ago tomorrow. The first thing we did was go to our cabin, which is a two-bedroom suite. The two bedrooms plus the living room combined are the size of a large coffee table. But it would be fine, Laurie assured me, because we would rarely be in the room. There was too much fun to be had on the ship, and I, Andy Carpenter, am nothing if not fun loving.

Almost immediately we were directed to find our life jackets and make it to our assigned stations, which were listed on the door. I'm not a big fan of needing life jackets because by definition they imply danger to life. That's why, for example, we don't keep life jackets in our den at home.

I could barely figure out the various straps to get mine on, so Ricky helped me. And of course I was under no stress during this drill; the chance that I would be able to manage it while on the deck of a sinking ship is infinitesimal.

We did as instructed and made it to our station. Once there we stood with maybe two hundred other life-jacketed passengers and responded when our names were called. One of the crew assured us that if a passenger was not there to answer to his or her name, another crew member would be sent to their stateroom to get them. This was a mandatory drill.

After the roll call, we were told that in an emergency we were to do what we had just practiced: grab our life jackets and come to these stations. Lifeboats would then be lowered automatically from high up on the ship down to us, and we would get in. The plan, I suppose, was to then happily row away to the sounds of Celine Dion coming from the sinking ship's audio system.

Almost immediately I recognized a problem. I think I read somewhere that some of the *Titanic* lifeboats never even got used, and they didn't have to come down on elevators. They were just sitting there on the side of the ship. So in our case, the ship would be sinking rapidly, but all the lifeboat elevators would work perfectly? Unlikely at best.

I was thinking maybe two-thirds of them would make it down. Doing the math, that meant that one-third wouldn't, leaving a lot of people floating around, boatless. I do not envision my final resting place to be at the bottom of the ocean, surrounded by rusting buffet tables.

It wasn't mentioned, but my guess was that the crew still clung to the antiquated notion that women and children have priority. That is so yesterday.

I'm fine with Laurie and Ricky getting special status, but it shouldn't be a blanket policy. It represents sexism and ageism; two isms that I am firmly opposed to. Sinkism and drownism are two more.

So I could see I was going to be left having to fend for myself against the other men on board. Some of them were really old, so I figured I could outrun or even outfight them. But others looked in good shape, so I'd have to outthink them. I hadn't come up with a strategy, but putting on one of Laurie's dresses and lipstick was a possibility.

Laurie could tell that I wasn't approaching this with the right attitude, so she starting telling me about the glorious diversions the ship offered: "Andy, there are an amazing amount of things to do. There are restaurants, bars, a bowling alley, bingo games, shows, movies, a casino, arcades, a library, computers, amusement rides, swimming pools, and, best of all, a close-up view of the ocean."

"That's great," I said. "But you know what else has all of those things? New Jersey. And you can't slip and fall off New Jersey. You can stand on a street corner in Paterson for ten years and never get seasick or need a lifeboat."

The truth is that the week has been relaxing and bearable. We've made stops at five Caribbean islands. They were all exactly the same; I'm pretty sure that we really went to the same island five times. They just called it by different names, and they cleverly changed the T-shirts in the stores, but I saw through the ruse.

Thanksgiving was last week, but the ship is in Christmas mode. Decorations are everywhere, Santas are there to "Ho, ho, ho" at every kid that walks by, and Christmas music is piped throughout.

I can usually stand Christmas music for about an hour, and then I want to scream when it's played. Of course, Laurie thinks the Christmas season lasts for four months, so I've been hearing it since Halloween. It doesn't take me long to get sick of Bing Crosby telling me that Santa knows when I've been sleeping and when I'm awake.

The island shops were also decorated for Christmas, which seemed completely incongruous. It felt like 145 degrees outside, and all the windows were decorated with fake snow, candy canes, and tinsel.

Time on the ship itself has been reasonably enjoyable; Ricky has had plenty to do, while Laurie and I have been resting and reading. We've also been doing our fair share of drinking, though it's embarrassing that every drink I order comes with a little umbrella in it.

Laurie and Ricky wanted to play bingo yesterday. I agreed because I am an agreeable guy, but I had one condition: if I won, either she or Ricky had to be the one to yell "Bingo!" I won the first game, and Ricky, who does not share my fear of humiliation, happily screamed it out.

We did have one disaster happen. On Sunday, I went into the bar area to watch pro football, but the only sports station that the ship gets is ESPN. There are no afternoon football games on ESPN, so instead I watched bass fishing, just so I could see the updated NFL scores scrolling across the bottom of the screen. A guy next to me at the bar tried to engage me in bass-fishing talk. It was not my finest moment.

Right now we're close to pulling into port on the West Side of Manhattan, so I turn on my cell phone, and I see that I have six messages, all from Willie Miller, and all in the last four hours.

Each message is almost identical: "Andy, it's Willie. Tara and Sebastian are good, but I need to talk to you about something else. It's important. But Tara and Sebastian are really good."

Tara is my golden retriever, best friend, and greatest living creature on the face of the earth, or any other planet known or still to be discovered. Sebastian is our basset hound, also a great dog, but, candidly, not in Tara's class. There is nothing and no one else in Tara's class.

I'm a defense attorney, and Willie is my friend and former client. He and his wife, Sondra, are my partners in the Tara Foundation, our dog-rescue operation. They are also taking care of Tara and Sebastian while we are away, and Willie is smart enough to realize that if he left an urgent message without assuring me of their good health, I would freak out.

As soon as I have enough bars on my phone, I call him.

"Andy, are you back?" he asks, in lieu of "Hello."

"Almost. Tara and Sebastian are okay?" I know he said they were, but I seem to need further reassurance.

"They're good. Can you meet me at the Passaic County jail in an hour?"

"You're in jail?"

"No . . . I'm home." Then, "I've got a better idea. How about if I meet you in front of your house and we can go down there together? In an hour?"

"I can't get there that fast, Willie. I'm still on the ship."

"Then make it two hours. Thanks, Andy."

Click.

He's hung up before I have a chance to ask why he wants me to go down to the jail, which means I have two hours of blissful ignorance to savor.

There is no way this can be good," I say, once we're in the car.

"I hope he didn't lose his temper with a potential adopter," Laurie says.

Willie can be volatile, and he has no patience for anyone who comes in to adopt a dog but then demonstrates a lack of respect for it. If he doesn't think they would represent a good home for one of our dogs, he can be rather confrontational and blunt about it.

People don't like to be told that they aren't worthy of adopting a dog, but most of them have the good sense not to argue with Willie. A few have tried to, and that's when it can get ugly.

Christmas is a particularly dangerous time in this regard, since people are inclined to get dogs as gifts, like a tennis racquet, or a toaster oven. People should be looking for a member of the family, not something that they can unwrap and return. Willie is keenly aware of this, and protective of the dogs in our care.

"I don't think so," I say. "He was in control of when he

was going to go to the jail; he wasn't being dragged there by the police."

"Maybe someone he knows is there."

"That's what I'm afraid of." I don't have to explain what I mean; I've been trying to avoid taking on clients for a long time, but it never seems to work out. Willie calling me down to the jail has raised my anti-client alert system to DEFCON 1.

"What does Uncle Willie want, Dad?" Ricky asks from the backseat.

"I don't know, Rick. Maybe a favor of some kind."

"He's your friend, right?"

"Yes."

"And he does favors for you, right?"

I turn to Laurie. "Do you have a sock or something you can put in his mouth?"

Instead, she says, "Yes, Rick. Uncle Willie does many favors for Dad. They are good friends."

We get to our house on Forty-second Street in Paterson, New Jersey. I've lived here almost my whole life, and it always feels great to come back home when I've been away. The Christmas tree in the living room is visible from the street, and the decorative lights on it are turned on. Laurie somehow knows how to do that from her phone; I wouldn't have the slightest idea how.

Willie is waiting out in front, holding Tara and Sebastian on leashes. Laurie, Ricky, and I get out of the car and spend the next few minutes petting and rolling on the ground with the two of them. Actually, Sebastian doesn't roll, but a couple of times he almost tips over. It's good that he doesn't because it would take a crane to get him up.

It is amazingly good to see them, and judging by the speed at which their tails are wagging, they are more than a little glad to see us. I would like this reunion to last forever, mainly so I won't have to talk to Willie about the favor involving the jail. But it's cold out here, so we need to move this along.

I delay the conversation with Willie further by carrying the bags in, but once that's done, Willie asks, "Andy, remember my friend Tony Birch?"

"No."

"You remember, Tony Birch," he coaxes. "Tony? Tony Birch?"

"I don't, Willie. So why don't you just tell—"

He interrupts, not giving up. "Anthony. Anthony Birch. We call him Tony."

"You mean Tony Birch?" I ask, changing tactics.

"Yeah, that's him."

"I don't remember him, Willie. But why are we talking about him?"

"We were cellmates for a while. Great guy; I know I mentioned him to you."

"Is he still in jail?" I ask.

"He got out years ago, but he just got arrested again. They said he murdered a guy."

"So you want me to find him a lawyer?" I ask, on the off chance that if you say something out loud, even something stupid, that might make it come true.

"I want you to be his lawyer. He needs you, Andy. He would never hurt anybody."

"You said he was your cellmate. What was he in for back then?"

"Manslaughter."

"This is the guy who would never hurt anybody?" I ask, as gently as I can.

"He didn't do it, Andy."

"Didn't do which? The manslaughter or the murder?"

"Both."

Ricky's words are ricocheting around inside my skull. *He's your friend, right? And he does favors for you, right?*

When I get Ricky alone, I'm going to scream really loudly at him, but the undeniable truth is that he's right. Willie has always been there for me, and I've called on him many times. He has even saved my life while risking his own life.

"When was he arrested?" I ask.

"Yesterday."

"And he doesn't have a lawyer yet?"

"They gave him a public defender."

"The public defenders are terrific."

"Not as good as you. Tony wants you. He knows we're friends."

I have nowhere to go with this. I'm trapped. "Okay, let's go. I'll talk to Tony Birch."

"He's a great guy."

"I'm not committing to anything right now other than talking to him. Okay?"

"Got it," Willie says, though I know he paid no attention to what I said. "You'll like him. You won't be sorry."

I'm already sorry is what I think but don't say. The other thing I think as we head for the jail is that I'd rather be playing bingo.

The only positive thing about visiting the jail is that they're not piping in Christmas music.

But it is a relentlessly depressing place to be, regardless of the season. I know, because I have spent more time in this place than most convicted felons.

"My man Willie came through."

Those are the first words that Tony Birch says when he's brought into the lawyer's visiting room. He doesn't look much more than thirty years old; he has jet-black hair and is built like a tight end for the Giants. Although I can't ever remember seeing a Giants tight end in handcuffs, even though some of them occasionally play like it.

"You seem surprised," I say.

"I'm always surprised when somebody does what they say they're going to do. Although in Willie's case, not so much. That's why I called him."

"I told him I would talk with you. No commitments beyond that."

"Fair enough; I appreciate the opportunity. Let's talk."

"Okay. I've just gotten back from a vacation to nowhere,

so I don't know anything about your situation. Tell me whatever you think is relevant."

He nods. "Three days ago a guy, Frankie Zimmer, was found dead on Bergen Street in Paterson. I'm told he was shot in the back of the head. Yesterday they arrested me."

"Did you know the victim?"

He nods. "We grew up together. We . . . hung out . . . on the same streets downtown."

Something about the way Tony says "hung out" strikes me. "What does 'hung out' mean? You sang on the street corner together? You were on the same bowling team?"

"We were in a gang. We called ourselves the Fulton Street Boyz. *Boyz* with a *z*."

"Why the *z*?"

He shrugs. "I never figured that out."

"So let me guess. You lived on Fulton Street."

"Actually no. But a bunch of the guys did. Anyway, we did some stupid stuff."

"When did you get out of prison?"

"Three years ago. I had a five-year sentence for involuntary manslaughter; got paroled in three."

"What have you been doing since then?"

"I'm a mechanic. I worked for a guy for two years and then bought the shop when he retired. I've been doing okay."

"The involuntary manslaughter conviction; what were the circumstances?"

"I got in a street fight; a guy attacked me. I defended myself and threw a punch. It knocked the guy back into the street and he got killed by a car."

"Self-defense?"

Tony nods. "Yeah. But a couple of guys saw it differently, and they testified against me. Guys that I thought were my friends." He pauses for a moment before dropping the bomb. "One of those guys was Frankie Zimmer."

"Frankie Zimmer testified against you?" I don't know what evidence the police have, but they obviously won't have a problem with motive.

"Yeah."

"And he was lying?"

"Yeah."

"So the police think you got out, waited three years, and then got your revenge?"

Tony shrugs. "I guess so."

"I assume you don't have an alibi to show you were somewhere else at the time and place of the murder?"

"I don't even know when he was killed, or where. They haven't told me anything, and my lawyer said I shouldn't talk to them."

"Excellent advice. Who's your lawyer?"

"Hopefully you. But right now it's a public defender . . . Ellen Richter. She seemed nice enough."

I know Ellen; she's a dedicated and talented attorney. "She's a good lawyer."

"She's not you."

"How do you know so much about me?"

"Willie talks about you a lot, and I got a rescued dog from you guys. Zoey . . . she's the greatest dog ever. I miss her already."

I don't have a mirror with me, but I think my ears literally perk up at the mention of this dog, though I don't remember her.

"What kind of dog?"

He smiles. "I'm embarrassed to say, but she's a Nova Scotia duck-tolling retriever."

"Seriously?"

He nods. "Yeah. I had no idea what she was, so I did one of those DNA tests and sent it in. Go figure . . . a Nova Scotia duck-tolling retriever in Paterson, New Jersey. There must be a story behind that."

"Where is Zoey now?"

"Willie has her."

"Good. He'll take good care of her."

"Will you take the case?"

"I haven't decided, but I'll look into it and let you know what I decide. For now Ellen is more than capable of taking you through the arraignment."

"I don't have much money, and my business isn't worth a whole lot without me there to run it. I only have one other employee."

This gets better and better. "I understand. My decision will have nothing to do with money, that much I can assure you."

"So what will you base your decision on?"

"What I learn about your case, and about you. And . . ."

"And what?"

I shouldn't say it, but I go ahead and tell him the truth anyway. "Whether or not I can bring myself to say no to Willie."

've recently adjusted my career goal.

For the last few years, I've been intent on not having a career. But despite my vow not to take on clients, for one reason or another I always seem to wind up with them. So the pattern has been that I then renew my retirement vow, only to get stuck once again with a new client.

I've never been big on self-introspection, or even self-awareness. I don't even take selfies. Pretty much the only self I can identify with is self-ish.

So as a rule I don't dig too deep, maybe because I'm afraid of what I might find, or maybe because I'm afraid I won't find anything. I'm not sure if either of those are true, and I don't much care anyway. I'm sure I must have some hidden feelings, but I'm not about to go poking around, looking for their hideout.

But I did have an uncharacteristic revelation recently. I had been thinking that my retirement dream stemmed from laziness. I am quite wealthy, from an inheritance and some lucrative cases. So with the profit motive no longer a factor, I just naturally assumed that my desire to avoid work came from a yearning for a life of leisure.

But that's not it, or at least that's not all of it.

I'm actually afraid to work. I'm afraid of a lot of things, but I had never realized that work was high up on the list. I've learned that it is.

Once I became wealthy and didn't need to earn more money, I decided to only represent people that I believed to be innocent. I understand that I could be wrong, but that's a risk I'm willing to take. The risk that scares the shit out of me is having an innocent client and not being able to convince a jury of that truth.

That failure would inevitably lead to a person's spending most or all of the rest of their life in jail for a crime they did not commit, all because their lawyer couldn't get twelve people to see the truth. That would be really tough for me to live with.

So, bottom line, that's a key reason for my not wanting to work anymore, and why I have to be dragged kicking and screaming into a courtroom. When I'm afraid of something, I avoid doing it. It's a logical reaction, and logic is my stock-in-trade.

But it was Laurie who effectively weakened my resistance. Not by helping me overcome my fear; the next fear I overcome will be the first. No, instead she diabolically used her own logic to defeat me.

She pointed out that if I saw myself as retired and dead set on not taking clients, then every time I wound up with one, I would feel like a failure. And since I naturally hate feeling like a failure, I was generally miserable.

So she suggested I see myself as semiretired. I could still resist clients, and when I was successful in that resistance, that was great. But when I was forced to take one on, that would be less painful because it would fit into my semiretired status.

That made sense to me; I even considered printings business cards that say ANDY CARPENTER, SEMIRETIRED ATTORNEY-AT-LAW. But I didn't, because business cards are used to attract clients, and I don't want any damn clients.

Which brings me to Tony Birch.

"What did you think of him?" Laurie asks.

"My assessment is he's either a murderer, or not."

"Well, that narrows it down."

"He's done time for manslaughter, and the cops obviously think they have evidence that he committed this murder, for which he had motive. Until we see the evidence, that's the reason to think he's a murderer."

"And the reason not to?"

"Willie believes in him. I can't think of too many times that Willie has been wrong about people."

"And he's your friend."

Laurie knows my definition of friendship contains one abiding principle: a friend is always there for you, no matter what. You can not see a friend for months at a time, you can insult them mercilessly, you can be totally uninterested in the events of their lives, but when they need you, you step up. And they step up for you.

Willie and I step up for each other; we always have.

"Yes, he's my friend," I say. "And he just about begged me to do this."

Ricky comes into the room. "Hi, Dad."

"It's all your fault," I say.

"What did I do?"

"You're growing up too fast."

"What's he talking about, Mom?"

Laurie shakes her head. "Don't you worry about it, Rick. You keep growing up as fast as you want."

Ricky nods, as if he considers that completely reasonable. "Okay." With that, he goes to the refrigerator, takes out a bunch of grapes, and goes back to his room.

"So what are you going to do?" Laurie asks.

"I was hoping you'd decide for me."

She shakes her head. "Can't help you with that. But if you take the case, you'll be out of the house a lot, so you won't have to hear as much Christmas music."

"That would be a plus." I pause. "I've made my decision."

"And that is?"

"I've decided to ask you to tell Willie that I don't want to take the case."

She shakes her head, which is not exactly a major surprise. "No chance."

"What if I buy you a really nice gift?"

"No."

"How about a three-month, around-the-world cruise? We can leave Friday and play bingo every day."

"Andy . . ."

"All right. I'll think some more."

Tony Birch said he thought you'd take his case," Ellen Richter says. "Knowing you as I do, I just assumed he was delusional. But since you're sitting here, maybe he wasn't."

"Hopefully he was," I say. "He and I have a good friend in common, and that friend asked me to get involved. I know very little about it so far, and if you think I'm stepping on your toes, I'll happily back off."

"Step all you want. You'd be making my day, my month, and Billy would nominate you for the cover of *Public Defender Magazine*."

Billy is Billy "Bulldog" Cameron, who has been in charge of the Passaic County Public Defender's office for as long as I can remember. About twenty minutes after he got the job, he started complaining about how understaffed and underfunded the office was, and he hasn't stopped since. Of course, he was right then and he is right now, and he's been right all the years in between.

Billy would definitely be delighted to be able to hand off the Tony Birch case to me, as would Ellen. In any event, it wouldn't matter. If I want the case, the choice would be left with the client, and he has already made his preference clear.

"So tell me what you can about the case," I say.

Ellen has to be a bit careful here since I have not been hired by Tony Birch. That means there are privilege considerations.

"What do you know so far?"

"The name of the victim and the fact that Birch had reason to have a grudge against him. I also know from Birch that he is claiming innocence of both this and the involuntary manslaughter charge which put him in jail in the first place."

She nods. "I actually don't know much more than that. The victim, Frankie Zimmer, was found by a bartender as he was closing up the other night, down on Bergen Street. He took a bullet to the back of his head, apparently as he was walking home. Two days later they arrested Birch."

The speed with which the arrest was made is worrisome. It doesn't sound like there were eyewitnesses who would have tied Birch to the murder. Cops and prosecutors don't like to be accused by defense attorneys of rushing to judgment, so for them to have moved this quickly, they must be confident.

"What else do they have on him besides motive?"

"I honestly don't know; we're still waiting on the discovery. But they sure seem confident."

"Who's the prosecutor?"

"Stan Godfrey. Do you know him?"

"He's an asshole."

She nods. "You obviously know him."

"Actually I don't, but that seems to be the unanimous point of view."

Godfrey is considered an up-and-comer in the prosecutor's office. He's in his midthirties, and though I've never tried a case against him, he's said to be both excellent and arrogant, not necessarily in that order. I don't know what his career goals are, but the word is that he thinks he should be sitting in the governor's mansion next week.

"So no plea deal offers?" I ask, although I'm quite sure it's too soon for that to have taken place.

"Not yet; no conversations of any kind. I just don't know enough, and Birch volunteered that he wasn't interested anyway."

"What did you think of him?"

She pauses a while to consider her answer. "First impression, I liked him. Seemed reasonable and fairly intelligent. He's a guy who got out of prison and was making a life for himself. Started a business, stayed out of trouble for three years."

"Awful long time to wait to get his revenge."

She nods. "That's my view also. Something about it doesn't seem right, but they must have significant evidence to make them move so quickly. Of course, they could be right. Maybe Birch ran into Zimmer on the street, and it triggered all the old feelings. I really can't say at this point."

"When is the arraignment?"

"Tomorrow at ten a.m. You going to be there? Because if you are, I'd consider it an early Christmas present, and I can make a spa appointment for myself."

I laugh. "I might be there, but if I am, it will be as a spectator."

"So are you going to take on the case? The suspense is killing me."

"Sorry. I'm just not ready to pull the trigger on this."

She nods. "I understand. You know, I had heard a while back that you were retiring."

"I heard the same thing. Apparently it was just a rumor. A wonderful, glorious rumor."

Willie is already sitting in the first row when I enter the courtroom.

Ellen Richter is alone at the defense table. The two chairs next to her are empty; Tony Birch hasn't been brought in yet. Only three people are in the gallery, besides Willie and me. This case is not exactly a media sensation. One ex–gang member accused of killing another is not quite the Kennedy assassination.

Across the way there are three people, two men and a woman, standing next to the prosecution's table. The two men are both in their thirties, but I've got a pretty good guess which one is Stan Godfrey. He looks confident and in control, exuding an arrogance that reminds me of something I once heard my grandmother say. In referring to a neighbor who flaunted her wealth, she said that the woman acted "like her shit doesn't smell."

My grandmother was a really cool lady.

I take the seat next to Willie, who says, "Hey, Andy." If he's surprised to see me, he's hiding it well.

"You knew I'd be here?"

"Yup."

"How did you know?"

"Because I asked you to, and you're my friend."

Willie has a way of making everything simple; he would have flunked out of law school.

Ellen Richter turns and sees me. She puts her hand on the back of one of the empty chairs and says, "I saved you a seat. You can see better from up here."

I nod in resignation and sit down at the defense table. A few minutes later, Tony Birch is led in by the bailiffs. He sees me and smiles, but doesn't say anything. Then he turns to Willie and offers a thumbs-up.

Ellen has a right to be annoyed by what must feel like a denigration of her worth, but she's smiling wider than Tony. She knows she's about to put this case in the "not my problem" file.

Judge Neal Baron enters and we all rise as the bailiff instructs. I've tried two cases before Judge Baron. It goes without saying that he finds me annoying and obnoxious; all judges seem to feel that way. I'm just speculating here, but I think it's probably because when I'm in a courtroom, I am annoying and obnoxious. There are even some people who would be inclined to remove *when I'm in a courtroom* from the previous sentence.

But Judge Baron is smart and fair even to those he finds annoying and obnoxious, and he even occasionally uses sarcasm effectively, so I'm pleased that he's presiding. There's no guarantee it will be his case when and if this ultimately goes to trial, but the chances are good.

He gavels the proceedings to order and is about to speak when he notices me at the defense table and stops. Then, "Mr. Carpenter, my records do not show that you

28

are participating in this case. Are you just auditing the trial? Attempting to pick up pointers? To what do we owe this honor?"

"With Your Honor's permission, I'm a late addition to the defense team."

Ellen says, "And with Your Honor's permission, at the conclusion of this arraignment, I am a late subtraction from the defense team."

"I need a lineup card to keep track," Judge Baron says dryly. "Let's proceed."

The arraignment proceeds smoothly, as arraignments generally do. Godfrey summarizes the charges against Tony, using approximately twice as many words as necessary. This is a guy who likes to hear himself talk.

Ellen makes a request for bail, which Godfrey opposes and which has absolutely no chance of success. Judge Baron swats it away like a fly. Then all three of us rise when Tony is asked to enter his plea, and his 'Not guilty, Your Honor' is said in a firm, decisive tone. Ellen coached him well.

It's all over in less than twenty minutes. I haven't said a word because I'm not officially part of the defense team yet, and because there is nothing I could add anyway.

The bailiff comes to take Tony back to the jail, and I say, "I'll come see you tomorrow."

"Thanks," he says, and then turns to Ellen. "I appreciate all you've done. Believe me, this is not a reflection on you." It's a gracious thing to say and elevates him a bit in my eyes.

"Good luck to you, Tony," Ellen says. "You're in good hands."

I walk back to Willie, who is waiting for me. "You didn't do much."

I nod. "I'm pacing myself."

"Tony's got a really cool dog; he rescued her from us a couple of years ago. Some kind of Novia Scotia something. Her name is Zoey."

"He told me."

"She's going to stay at our house. That makes three, but Sondra doesn't mind, and we've got plenty of room. You want to come see her now?"

"I can't . . . I've got lawyer stuff to do. Is Zoey doing okay?"

"She's bummed. Moping around. I guess she misses Tony. But she'll be okay." Then, "Andy, I don't think Tony has enough money to pay you."

"He was very up-front about that."

"I'll cover it."

Willie has plenty of money. He was wrongly imprisoned for seven years, and when I got him out on appeal, he made a large sum of money from a civil suit we filed against the rich people who had framed him. He's also been lucky with investments since then.

"Willie, there is simply no possibility that I am going to take your money."

"I figured, but it would be good if you changed your mind. Tony's my friend; you shouldn't have to pay. How about we split it?"

"No, thanks."

"It's really important that you win."

"I'll try to remember that."

Usually at this point I gather our team together for a meeting.

It's always too early to form a coherent strategy; I just like them to realize the job we have ahead of us. I tell them who our client is and what we know about the case so far.

This time, however, I know virtually nothing, so I am going to put off the actual meeting. I'll just contact each of them, let them know what's going on, and tell them to be ready.

I hate this part. Laurie and I divvy up the phone calls to the team members. She calls her investigative team partners, Corey Douglas and Marcus Clark. They recently formed their own group since I don't take on enough cases to keep them busy. Laurie and Corey are both ex-cops, and Marcus is . . . well, more about Marcus later.

The fourth member of their group is Simon Garfunkel, Corey's ex K-9 partner, who eats more kibble than the rest of the group combined. But he's a hell of a good dog to have on our side. Besides, Tara likes him, and she's an even better judge of character than Willie. The presence of Simon is why they all call themselves the K Team.

I have three calls to make, so I follow my normal form and make the easiest one first. It's to Sam Willis, who is my accountant in real life, and our invaluable information gatherer on a case. Sam is a genius on a computer, able to hack into anything, anywhere. It's not often legal, and I'm not often bothered by that.

"Sam, we have a client."

"Yesssss," he says, stretching the word out and sounding more like Marv Albert than my accountant. Sam loves investigative work, though he chafes at only utilizing his considerable talents sitting in front of his computer screen. He thinks of himself as a cross between Bat Masterson and Batman.

"Our client is Tony Birch, and he's accused of murdering a guy named Frankie Zimmer. That is literally all I know, so please gather as much information as you can. For now, just search public information."

"I'm on it, Chief."

"I've told you before, Sam, I'm not a chief."

"Roger that."

"Roger says bye-bye." I hang up.

That was the fun call.

Next is Edna.

Edna is my office manager, or at least that's how she refers to herself. Edna does absolutely nothing; compared to her, I have an all-consuming work ethic. Since she gets paid whether we have a client or not, she does not exactly spend her time chasing ambulances.

I don't like disappointing people, probably born out

of my occasional experiences with girls in high school. Telling Edna we have a client is therefore unpleasant for me; hearing that she might have to work will crush her soul.

This time she takes it surprisingly well; she's almost fatalistic about it. "It's okay, Andy. I dreamt this would happen; I woke up the other night in a cold sweat. It's like when I dreamt that my aunt Sylvia had died, and then she passed away three weeks later."

"You're psychic."

"I know. Andy, I have just one question."

"What is it?"

"Is there any chance he'll cop a plea?"

"I don't know. But I'm not going to lie to you. I doubt it."

I can hear the sharp intake of breath as she absorbs this news. "It's okay, Andy. It's not your fault; these things happen."

The third call is the one I am dreading the most. It's to the other lawyer in my firm, Hike Lynch. Hike is an excellent attorney, but also the most depressing and pessimistic person on the planet. In his mind nothing is ever going to turn out well, and if it does, then that just doubles the chance that the next thing to come up will be a disaster.

I get Hike's answering machine at home, so I try him on his cell. He answers on the first ring with "Hey, Andy! I was just going to call you!"

He sounds upbeat, and I don't mean just for Hike. For Hike, soft sobbing would be upbeat. This sounds like normal-person upbeat. And a lot of commotion is in the background.

"What's going on, Hike? Where are you?"

"I'm at a party. Hey, guys! Hold it down a minute. It's my friend Andy."

"You're at a party? On Planet Earth?"

"South Carolina."

With those two words it instantly makes sense. A few years ago I sent Hike down to South Carolina in connection with a case, and he immediately executed a bizarre transformation. Not only did he turn into a happy-go-lucky, optimistic guy while he was down there, but he even made friends. I assumed a pod from some cheery planet had taken over his body, but I didn't complain because pod-Hike was a lot more pleasant to talk to.

Even more incredibly, the friendships Hike made down there have lasted; Hike has kept in touch with them, and they with him. Before the South Carolina connections, the longest-lasting friendship Hike ever had was twenty minutes.

"I didn't realize you were down there," I say. "I was calling to tell you that we have a client."

There's a few seconds of silence, although the sounds of partying in the background are still there. "I'm not coming back, Andy."

"It's okay, the case is just starting. Take your time."

"No, I mean I'm moving down here, for good. That's why I was going to call you. I'm getting married. Darlene said yes."

I've met Darlene; she visited Hike in New Jersey a few years ago, but then they broke off their relationship. Obviously it's been rekindled. Spending time with Darlene was an interesting experience; in terms of a sense of humor, she made Hike look like Will Ferrell.

"That's wonderful, Hike. You're going to start a law practice down there?"

"Nah, law brings me down. For now Darlene and I are going to laugh and enjoy life. We might even open a comedy club."

I don't know what to say to that, so I don't say anything. Instead I start thinking about anyone I know that can replace Hike. I ask Hike if he has any ideas.

"I'll have to think about it. Can I get back to you? The party is getting pretty wild; the karaoke is starting."

Hike doing karaoke and opening a comedy club is as likely as me putting on a tutu and dancing *Swan Lake.*

I wish Hike well and end the call.

Hike is not coming back. New Jersey will never be the same.

Many couples have traditions, special rituals that they share.

They can be small ones: perhaps always going to a certain restaurant on their birthdays. Or they can be more substantial: maybe buying a piece of jewelry, or going on a vacation to celebrate an event that is meaningful to both of them. They're often romantic and they serve to maintain closeness between them.

Laurie and I are no different, and we have one tradition that we particularly adhere to. It's for us and only us.

We go to murder scenes.

Sam Willis has provided me with everything the media has reported on the Zimmer murder. It's not a hell of a lot, but for the moment it's all we have to go by.

Frankie Zimmer was shot at one in the morning walking to his home after leaving the Crown Bar, on Bergen Street in Paterson. He took one bullet to the back of his head, killing him instantly. The assailant fled the scene and there were no eyewitnesses.

Early reports said that the police had a person of interest, though they did not identify him. Two days later an arrest was made, and Tony Birch was taken into custody. The police did not publicly state their reasons for believing Birch is their killer, and the truth is that there was no media pressure on them to do so. There was nothing high profile about this murder.

Zimmer was identified as an independent contractor. That could mean anything from a handyman who does odd jobs to a guy who has a company that builds buildings. I have a hunch he was closer to the former.

We have not gotten the discovery material yet, though I've put in a call to Godfrey's office asking for it. I've been promised it will start coming in tomorrow, and if it doesn't, I'll make a complaint to the judge. Godfrey knows that, so I expect him to follow through on his promise.

The phone call, and the possible complaint to the judge, are the kinds of things that Hike would ordinarily do. It reminds me that I need to focus on finding a replacement for him.

In the meantime, Laurie and I have driven downtown for a romantic walk. We're going to do it in reverse, starting at the address we have for Zimmer's home and walking to the bar.

I have on occasion dreaded walks with Laurie because she treats them like exercise regimens. When it's just her and me and we have no goal other than to walk, she keeps up a ridiculous pace, and it can feel like a near-death experience.

I've been known to fake an injury to get her to slow down. Once I fake-sprained my ankle, but later in the day I forgot which ankle I was supposed to limp on, and she caught me.

In this case, we're going slowly to observe our surroundings, though at least for now there's nothing relevant to the case to observe. We're walking along the half of the route that Zimmer never even got to that night. We're just trying to get a feeling for the area; somehow that seems to bring me more into a case.

About halfway to the bar we arrive at the murder scene. It's not hard to identify since police tape is still up and a cop is guarding it. I'm not sure why this is necessary; I'm certain they must have gotten all the forensic information from it that they're going to get.

Laurie knows the cop, and he brightens when he sees her. Laurie is extraordinarily easy to like, which comes in handy in her profession. She introduces him to me; his name is Fred Bixler. He doesn't sneer or scowl at me, which means he doesn't recognize my name. In Paterson, they actually teach a course at the Police Academy called Sneering at Andy Carpenter. The advanced class is called Giving Andy Carpenter the Finger. It's usually standing room only.

"How did it go down, Fred?" Laurie asks.

"Are you working the case?"

She nods. "Yes. On the defense side."

He doesn't seem put off by that. "The victim was walking in this direction and took one bullet in the back of the head. He fell over there, against the wall."

"Close-up shooter?"

Bixler shakes his head. "Looks like he was back behind that wall." He points to a spot about ten feet away.

"Pretty tough shot if the victim was moving," Laurie

says, then looks up and around us to check for street-lights. There are none close by. "And in the dark."

"That's for sure," Bixler says. "Does that fit with your client?"

She shrugs. "Don't know yet."

The conversation has taken place and come to a natural conclusion without my intervention becoming necessary; all I've had to do is smile and look pretty.

Once we're far enough away from Bixler, I say, "I hope Birch wasn't an Olympic shooting champion."

We continue our walk, learning absolutely nothing but getting a feel for the neighborhood. This is not exactly Rodeo Drive; it's mostly bars and liquor stores, with an occasional pawnshop and convenience store thrown in. It is not a street that I would be walking down at one o'clock in the morning, unless I was with Marcus Clark.

We reach the Crown Bar, which looks like every other bar in the neighborhood. The neon sign in front has a letter out, so it reads C OWN BAR, but I am able to figure it out. I'm a master investigator.

"You want to go in?" Laurie asks.

"Might as well."

So we go inside; the place redefines *seedy*. Only three customers are spread out along the bar. I don't like to make rash judgments, but if you're sitting in the Crown Bar at three o'clock in the afternoon, the chances are you're not waiting for a board of directors meeting to start.

The bartender looks at us with absolutely no interest at all. "What'll it be?" he asks, in a tone that says he couldn't care less what it will be, or if it will be anything.

"How's the Chilean Sea Bass today?" I ask.

Laurie rolls her eyes. She has developed different levels of eye rolls in response to my comments, depending on how sarcastic and obnoxious they are. I grade them on a ten-point scale; one means they barely budge, ten means they just about do a complete circle. This one is a six.

"What?" he asks. This guy is not going to be a bantering match for me.

Laurie takes over. "Were you working the night that Frankie Zimmer was killed?"

"Who wants to know?"

"We do."

"I was here," he says grudgingly.

"Did anything unusual happen that night? Anything that might relate to the murder?"

"I talked to the cops."

The guy is already annoying me, so I jump in. "That would be a good answer if the question had been 'Who did you talk to?' But that's not what the lady asked."

He thinks for a moment. "I've got nothing to say." Then he looks me straight in the eye. "So beat it."

With that he turns and walks to the other end of the bar, ending what can only be described as an incredibly enlightening interview.

"You taught him a lesson," Laurie says.

I nod. "Sometimes I can be too intimidating. So, do you want to leave, or do you want to try the Chilean Sea Bass?"

I drop Laurie off at home and head down to the Tara Foundation.

I can't stay long, but I want to meet Birch's dog, Zoey. I basically want to meet all dogs, but in this case I also want to be able to accurately tell him that I saw her and she's okay. I've also never seen a Nova Scotia duck-tolling retriever before.

Willie is at the supermarket when I get there, which I'm sort of pleased about. He'd no doubt ask me if I'd won Birch's case already; Willie doesn't have a fully developed understanding of the legal system.

His wife, Sondra, is there, as she seemingly always is. She's probably even more devoted to the dogs than either Willie or me.

"We bring her here most days," she says. "We're hoping she'll play with the other dogs, but so far she doesn't want to. I think she misses her owner."

I take Zoey into the adoption room, and within three minutes I'm in love. She comes over and puts her head on my knee, a sure signal for me to pet her head and scratch her chest. Tara does the same thing, but Tara doesn't seem sad. Zoey seems sad; I wish I could make her feel better.

I spend about ten minutes with her, petting her and telling her that no matter what happens, I promise she will be fine. I don't know if she understands, just like I never really know if Tara understands, but Zoey does seem to smile a little.

I thank Sondra and leave, heading down to the jail. I briefly debate whether to ask Laurie to come with me. I'd like her to hear Birch's story firsthand, especially since she generally has a more sensitive and accurate bullshit detector than I do. That's probably because she lives with me, so is exposed to it more.

I decide to go it alone because I have a feeling Birch will be more willing to open up to me without anyone else there.

It only takes me twenty minutes to navigate the system and be brought into the meeting room. That is historically quick, which I am pleased about. Every minute waiting at the prison feels like sixty.

Tony doesn't look as panicked as most clients in this situation, no doubt because he's been through it before. That doesn't mean he's less afraid; his previous experience with this predicament had him wind up in prison. If he loses this second time, there won't be a third. He will likely go away for the rest of his life. I'm sure he knows that.

"How's it going?" I ask, when he's seated and handcuffed to the metal table. I find that the guards here are not particularly trusting.

He shrugs. "Beats Rahway, but that's not saying much."

Rahway is the New Jersey state prison where I assume

he was incarcerated for the manslaughter conviction. It's not actually called Rahway anymore; it's now East Jersey State Prison. The name was changed in 1988, but everyone still calls it Rahway, even people like Birch who were barely born when the change was made.

Further complicating the matter is that the prison is not even actually in Rahway, but that geographical kernel of information doesn't seem to have much effect on the lives of the prisoners crammed in there.

"Let's try and keep you from going back there," I say. "Start by telling me all about your relationship to Frankie Zimmer."

"We were a bunch of assholes that thought the world owed us something, so we formed a gang. There were eleven of us, ten after Joey . . ."

He's paused, so I ask, "'Ten after Joey' what?"

"Joey Avera. He and his sister, Katy, were shot to death."

"What were the circumstances?"

"Some kind of home invasion. They never caught whoever did it."

"Okay. Go on. You and Frankie were part of this gang. Did you commit crimes?"

He hesitates, so I say, "You can tell me. I'm sure you know I'm not allowed to say a word to anyone."

"Yeah, we did some stuff." I don't respond, and he understands he needs to explain himself. "Some burglaries, and we strong-armed some people who didn't pay up."

"Pay up for what?"

"Gambling, drugs, whatever. Didn't much matter to us."

"You didn't know what they owed money for?"

David Rosenfelt

"We did what we were told."

"By who?"

He hesitates again. Then, "You need to think of us as a minor-league team, okay? We all wanted to make it to the majors. I know it's stupid, looking back, but . . ."

"You're not answering my question, Tony. Who were you working for?"

"The Blood Dragons."

I've heard of them; I was even part of a case where they were peripherally involved. They started in Passaic and have gradually expanded to control the street action in most of North Jersey. Their leader is a guy who goes by the name of Luther. That's it, just one name, like Cher or Madonna.

Luther is a dangerous character, violent in the extreme. He's been arrested a number of times, but witnesses tend to recant or disappear, and to my knowledge there have been no convictions.

"Did you have anything to do with Luther?"

Tony shakes his head. "Never met him. We were too far down the totem pole. We got our instructions from one of his people, Russell Estrada."

"Okay, we'll get into that later. Tell me more about Frankie Zimmer. You were in the same gang; does that mean you were friends?"

"I wouldn't say friends. But we knew each other, obviously, and we didn't have any problems."

I frown and shake my head; it's my less than subtle way of showing my frustration at the vague answers I'm getting. "But he was there the night that guy was killed, and he testified against you."

44

"Yeah."

Getting answers out of Tony is a bit like pulling teeth . . . molars. "I mean as part of the same gang, wasn't he breaking some kind of code?"

"Yeah. And not only that, he was lying."

I stand and start pacing around the room. I can tell that Tony is tense as well; if he wasn't chained to the table, we'd probably be circling each other in some weird interrogation dance. "Why would he have done that?"

"I never found out, and I tried. He stabbed me in the back."

"Could it be that he was just mistaken? Things happen fast in street fights."

Tony considers that for a few moments. "Possible, but I doubt it. And that wouldn't change the bottom line. We were supposed to back each other up."

I sit back down. "Did you ever confront him?"

Another hesitation. "I told him I was going to kill him."

"Did anyone hear you?"

Tony nods in what seems like resignation. "Yeah, people heard me. I did it in the courtroom."

When we were on the ship, I had made a promise to Ricky.

I had said that when we got home, I would take him to see the new animated Christmas movie from Disney. I said that because at the time I didn't know I'd be trying a murder case. I was also trying to trade that promise for permission from him and Laurie not to play bingo, but that didn't work out too well.

But as we get closer to trial, if there is one, it will be all-consuming. I know I will feel guilty about how little time I'm able to spend with Ricky, so I want to try to make up for it in advance. Besides, there are few people on the planet that I'd rather spend time with.

So, Disney movie it is.

The theater is a madhouse. The lobby feels like a human pinball machine, with kids bouncing off the walls. We wait on a ten-minute line for popcorn, candy, and sodas; based on the price, I should have gotten preapproval for a bank loan.

The move itself is quite tolerable, at least on the screen; there are a lot of references that I don't think kids will get, but adults like me actually do. Ricky sits to my left, and a father of a boy and a girl sits to my right. Which brings me to the problem . . .

The armrest.

The guy on my right, who I will heretofore refer to as "the enemy," seems to think that the armrest between us is his personal domain. Even worse, his large arm edges slightly over the surface area, into what is unquestionably my personal seat space.

Fortunately, when it comes to armrest wars, this is not my first rodeo. It's all a question of positioning and leverage; you need to get your elbow on the rear of the rest, closest to the back of the seats. That gives you a position of dominance; it's like having the high ground in a battle.

Just call this Popcorn Hill.

So I'm able to control the action from that position, though not without some difficulty. At one point I have to scratch my nose, no easy trick since I don't want to lose my right-elbow position, and I'm holding my soda in my left hand. But I get it done by letting Ricky hold my drink.

At one point the enemy has his left leg protruding into my space. It is clearly an attempt to open another skirmish, to try to draw my attention from the armrest conflict. I respond by doing my own stretch, hitting his leg while pretending it was an accident. He retreats in shame.

The war ends when for some reason his little daughter starts to cry, and they leave the theater. I wouldn't be surprised if he pinched her or something to make her cry, giving him cover to leave the battlefield without shame. The armrest, and total victory, are mine.

When we get home, I take Tara and Sebastian for their evening walk. If left to her own devices, Tara would walk at a fast pace; she's a multitasker who can walk and sniff at the same time. Sebastian, on the other hand, insists on walking slowly and ambling along. Hurrying, Sebastian apparently believes, is for suckers. When it comes to walking, Sebastian is to Tara as I am to Laurie.

While I sometimes talk to Tara at times like this, the truth is that she doesn't participate in the discussions. I don't even have any concrete evidence that she understands what the hell I'm talking about. But she stays by my side and seems to listen respectfully, which is all I care about. Talking out loud helps me to see things clearly.

"Tara, here's the situation. Our client had a motive to kill: the victim testified against him and effectively took away years of his life. Maybe he lied, or maybe he just saw the incident differently. But they were friends, so Tony views it as a betrayal.

"Unfortunately, he alerted the world, including a judge, prosecutors, bailiffs, and a courtroom full of people, that he was going to get revenge by killing the guy."

Tara doesn't respond, though I'm sure the gravity of the situation is sinking in. Golden retrievers are smart, and she would have graduated first in her class had she gone to canine college.

"But I haven't told you the worst part yet. There is no way the police would have arrested Tony if they didn't have much more evidence. Motive would never carry the day at trial; they aren't even required to demonstrate motive. When we see the discovery, we're going to find out they have a lot more."

I hadn't realized it, but a young couple is walking about twenty feet behind us. I don't know if they can hear me, but I decide to do the rest of my talking to myself. In days past they would have thought that I was a nut talking to myself; now with earpieces and smartphones people do it all the time.

The problem is that my internal voice doesn't sound any more upbeat than my external one. And a bit of resentment creeps into my conversation with myself. I don't want to have to be dealing with this stuff, but here I am. When we go for a walk in the park, I would rather talk to Tara about football or basketball.

I obviously have no idea what the defense strategy will be, since I don't know what the offense has in its arsenal yet. Maybe we'll be able to prove that Tony didn't do it or couldn't do it or wouldn't do it, but none of that is likely. If such an easy out existed, the prosecution wouldn't have moved so quickly and decisively.

So we'll likely be trying to demonstrate that there are other potential auditionees for the position of killer of Frankie Zimmer. Fortunately, that already holds some promise, even though we have barely scratched the surface. Zimmer was a gang guy, at least partially connected to Luther and the Blood Dragons.

This was not the campus Chess Club. It is not a stretch to imagine that members of those gangs could commit a murder; I have no doubt many of them have been there, done that. Whether we can tie one or more of them into this case enough to either demonstrate their guilt, or more likely get to reasonable doubt, is something I just have no way of knowing at this point. But at least it's a possibility.

About two blocks from the house, Sebastian does what he always does when we take the long walk. He decides he's had enough and camps his ass on the cement. When this first started happening, Tara always had a look on her face that said, *Why do we even bother with this dope?*

But that's changed ever since I came up with the idea of coaxing Sebastian along with biscuits. Sebastian would climb Mount Everest for a biscuit; walking two blocks is a breeze. Of course I can't give Sebastian biscuits without also giving them to Tara, so she's become more willing to tolerate her lazy brother.

When I finally get home, I head directly into Ricky's bedroom to tuck him in for the night. We always play a quick game of New York Giants football trivia, taking turns trying to stump each other.

Tonight it's his turn. "Dad, who is the Giants all-time scoring leader?"

"Tiki Barber?"

"Nope."

I think a little more. "Frank Gifford?"

"Nope."

I can see him starting his victory smile; it's my fatherly job to wipe it off his face. Fortunately for me, our rules allow for three guesses. "Is this touchdowns or total scoring? Do field goals and extra points count?"

"Yes," he says reluctantly, fearful that I have him now.

I've hit a nerve. "Pete Gogolak?"

"Dad . . ." It's his admission that I've won.

"Good try, Rick. But I am the master. You have much to learn from me."

I kiss him good night, and when I turn to leave, I see

Laurie standing in the doorway. She's watching us, and she's fighting back tears. She's really into the whole father-son relationship thing.

So am I.

What I didn't realize in my conversation with Tara and myself in the park was that I need to start looking at the big picture.

I've got a great son, I'm about to have a glass of wine and then get into bed with the love of my life, and I've got two fantastic dogs.

Maybe I should stop complaining about having a client.

Sam Willis calls at 10:00 A.M. to say that two cartons have been delivered to my office.

My office is on Van Houten Street in Paterson, on the second floor above Sofia Hernandez's fruit stand. I've been here since I opened my practice and was struggling, back when the discount I get on fresh fruit was meaningful. It's still fine for me, and I have just never had the desire to relocate. Sofia is my landlady, and she's such a nice and sensitive person that if I told her I was leaving, she'd be afraid she did something wrong.

Sam's office is down the hall from me, not directly above the stand, so the fresh cantaloupe aroma gets to me first in the morning. I think he's been secretly jealous of that since he moved in.

He was there when the boxes arrived, and since he has a key to my office, he took the delivery. Edna wasn't in because she's . . . Edna. The odds that the boxes might have arrived when she was there to accept them is . . . well, let's just say that Tony Birch has better odds of being declared innocent and receiving a handwritten apology and a gold watch from the governor.

I tell Sam that I'll be right down. I want to find out what the prosecution has on Birch; until I do, I'm frozen in place. This is one of those times when it would be helpful to have Hike go through it with me; but Hike is down in South Carolina singing karaoke and living the fun life.

He sent me the name of a lawyer he knows that he described as perfect for me. He ended the email with "Peace, Love, and Laughter, Hike." I cannot imagine what must be in the South Carolinian water. I've set up a lunch meeting with the guy he recommended. His name, Eddie Dowd, is familiar to me, but I can't place it.

I stop off on the way to pick up doughnuts and coffee for Sam and me. He likes the chocolate-cream filled and I like the vanilla. It's impossible to identify them from the outside, so I get three of each in separate bags. Then I write a little *V* on the vanilla bag. These are the little doughnut purchasing and eating techniques one picks up over time.

When I get to the office, I set up shop at my desk with the doughnuts, coffee, and discovery materials. I've barely taken a bite, I haven't even reached the cream part, when I start to realize the extent of the disaster. Tony Birch was at the Crown Bar the night that Zimmer was killed. Worse than that, he showed up early and asked for Zimmer by name. When told that Zimmer wasn't there, Tony loudly expressed his annoyance and left after forty-five minutes.

Obviously, the police believe that he kept an eye on the place, saw Zimmer show up, and then ambushed him on his way home.

It's a reasonable theory, and it gets considerably worse as I read on. A .38-caliber handgun was found buried in

Tony's backyard. It had no fingerprints on it; possibly it was wiped clean, or the person who used it and buried it wore gloves. The dirt would have made fingerprint retrieval difficult anyway.

However, it was wrapped in a handkerchief, and to complete the evidentiary trifecta, the handkerchief was analyzed and had DNA on it.

Tony Birch's DNA.

I remember that yesterday I was happy and content with my loving family and wonderful life. I was looking at the big picture, and in light of all that happiness it seemed silly and selfish to focus on the unhappy fact that I had a client.

But that was yesterday, and yesterday's gone.

I'm a defense attorney and certainly not one to look at any prosecution case and take it at face value. It's one side of the story, and my job is to present the other side. But I would be an idiot not to admit that the opposition's side, as represented in these documents, is daunting.

Also troubling is that Tony never mentioned to me that he was at the bar that night, if in fact he was. He would have to know that it was both relevant and incriminating, and he seemed smart enough to realize that it would certainly come out. Yet he withheld it from me. I don't know why, but I'm sure as hell not happy about it.

There are also a bunch of interviews that have already been done with witnesses to the threat Tony made on Zimmer's life in the courtroom.

The investigation has barely begun and I'm sure there will be other shoes to drop, small ones I hope. But what is already here is pretty bad. If uncontradicted, this evidence will carry the day.

I'm basically skimming through the documents, cringing as I read the bad news. I get through about two-thirds of them; a lot of the material consists of dry reports on the forensics. I have to leave because I'm meeting Eddie Dowd for lunch, and I can't say I'm sorry to interrupt this reading. If there is a pleasant part of it, I sure haven't gotten to it yet.

Unless Eddie Dowd turns out to be a pseudonym for Clarence Darrow, we've got a problem.

get to Charlie's Sports Bar about fifteen minutes early.

It's my favorite restaurant on earth, but I don't think I've had lunch here more than a handful of times. At night it's a different story; I have a regular table with my friends Pete Stanton and Vince Sanders, and I'm here quite often. Before I was married, I planted myself here pretty much every night.

The atmosphere is different at lunch because it's not as crowded, but mostly because there are no live sports on the many televisions scattered throughout. But the food is just as good, the beer just as cold, and the french fries just as crisp. And there are no Christmas decorations or Christmas music; Charlie's is Charlie's . . . no season or holiday changes that.

From my vantage point I have a view of the door, and I see a man come in and look around. My guess is he's Eddie Dowd, so I wave to him. He nods his understanding and comes toward me.

He's a huge guy, at least 270 pounds and six foot four. He's not in great shape and has a bit of a stomach, but he probably isn't more than twenty pounds overweight. He's got a large frame that can handle weight.

He's almost at the table, hand outstretched, when I realize why the name Eddie Dowd is familiar to me. "You played for the Giants," I say, shaking his hand.

He laughs. "You must be a fan; I was only there two years before I tore up my knee."

"I remember. Happened against the Colts. You made the tackle, but one of the Colts rolled into the side of your leg."

"Wow! That was eight years ago."

Eddie talks loudly and with enthusiasm. While not too many tables in the place are occupied, most of the people who are here are looking over at us.

He sits down and says, "I gotta tell you, I'm a big fan of yours. You've spiked a lot of balls in the end zone."

I just nod; I'm not sure how to answer that. "So after you left football you went to law school?"

"Yes, sir. Still can't believe I did that. I said to myself, 'Now what, Eddie?' And then I realized football was over and I needed to step up and make a play."

Between *spiking balls* and *making plays,* he seems to use a lot of football phrases. We talk some more; I'm more interested in talking about the Giants than lawyering, but I try to suppress that instinct.

He seems to know the law, and Hike says he's an excellent attorney. There's no way I can confirm that for sure while sitting here at Charlie's. I tell him that I have a case I'm working on, and that he is welcome to join the team for now, and then we'll revisit it after the end of the case.

"I get it," he says. "I'm on the practice squad, but I'll be ready to play when you put me in."

I hope he'll run out of football references before the trial. I tell him what the salary is for this case, and he seems more than happy with it. He'll come down to the office tomorrow for our team meeting and to go over the discovery.

"Wow, working with Andy Carpenter. I'll do whatever you say; you're the quarterback. You call the plays and I'll execute them."

He obviously reveres my ability as a lawyer, so he must be a smart guy. And I can talk about the Giants and football with him; all I could ever really talk about with Hike was disease and misery.

It's worth a shot.

I was going to go home after lunch and continue reading the discovery, but I change my mind and head to the jail. I can't put this off; it's client-confrontation time.

This time it takes me forty-five minutes to get in to see Tony, mainly because I hadn't called ahead. It's not necessary that I do, but doing so gets me on their schedule, and they are prepared. It's not exactly an operation that flourishes in spontaneity.

When Tony is brought in, he has a worried look on his face. "I didn't expect you back so soon. Is there anything new?"

"New to me, but not you. Why didn't you tell me that you went to the bar looking for Zimmer the night he was killed?"

He sags a bit . . . caught in the act. "I was afraid you

would decide not to take the case. I knew you'd find out about it eventually; the police had to have checked out the bar and talked to the bartender. But I hoped that by then you'd be well into the case, and that you would have come to believe me."

"So your plan was to get me to trust you by lying to me?"

He nods. "I wasn't lying; I was withholding."

That statement pisses me off, but I'm trying to control my anger. "For the purpose of this relationship, they are one and the same."

He nods. "Okay. I should have known better. I'm not the brightest client you've ever had."

"Tony, listen carefully. If you lie to me again, about anything . . . if you tell me you take two sugars in your coffee when you really take one . . . I'm going to resign from the case."

"I understand. It won't happen again."

"Why did you go to that bar looking for him?"

"He called me and said he wanted to meet me there."

"For what purpose?"

"He said he didn't want to talk about it on the phone. But that something had come up, relating to the old days, and that if we put our problems behind us, we could make a lot of money."

"You believed that?"

"No. I wouldn't believe him if he told me the sun was going to come up tomorrow. But he sounded different, maybe a little nervous, and I was curious and wanted to hear what he had to say."

"When was the last time you talked to him before that?"

Tony thinks for a moment. "Six, seven years. It was in that courtroom. I don't even know how he knew my cell phone number."

"So when you got to the bar, what happened?"

"Zimmer wasn't there, so I talked to the bartender and asked if he knew if he was coming in. He said he didn't know, so I waited for about forty-five minutes, had a few beers, and left. I was pissed off, mostly at myself for showing up in the first place."

"What did you do then?"

"I went home. I swear, Andy, I went home and went to sleep."

"Did you venture out into your backyard before you dozed off?"

"No . . . my backyard . . . what does that mean?"

"The murder weapon was buried back there."

I can tell by his expression that Tony is clearly stunned; if he's faking it, he's good enough to win a Tony. "Holy shit. Andy, this is no accident; someone is doing this to me. I'm being set up."

"They're doing a hell of a job." Then, "I've got an assignment for you."

"Okay. I've got some free time. But there can't be any traveling involved." He's trying to get back to his light-hearted attitude, but I can see it's hard. He's just realized beyond a doubt that he is being framed for murder; that's not conducive to humorous banter.

"I want you to write down everybody you knew back

in the days you were in the gang. I want to know what you did; leave nothing out. Also, tell me anyone you can think of that might have a grudge against you, and why."

"Okay. When do you need it?"

"Yesterday."

This is my second time at Charlie's today.

I'm okay with that; I could comfortably live the rest of my life on a burgers, wings, and fries diet. And with an NFL game on tonight, few places on the planet are more appealing. I've come a long way from watching bass fishing on the cruise, baby.

Pete Stanton and Vince Sanders are at our table when I get here. They are already knee deep in food and beer. Pete and Vince never learned the etiquette of waiting for everyone to arrive before starting a meal. They also never learned the etiquette of not wiping their mouths with their sleeves, or not burping into their beer.

Pete is captain of the Homicide Division of the Paterson Police Department, and Vince is the editor of the local newspaper. It would be a major news story worthy of a headline in Vince's paper if either of them ever picked up a check, but that is unlikely to happen anytime soon.

We barely have time to grunt hello, and it wouldn't matter because their mouths are full. But the game is about to start; Jacksonville is at Atlanta. Pete and Vince would happily watch any game, anytime. As much as I love football, I have to admit that if I haven't bet on the game, then I couldn't care less who wins. I don't bet much money, but just putting some on one side gives me a rooting interest and a reason for watching.

I bet on Jacksonville, and Atlanta is up by twenty-one at the half. Completely typical. That gives us fifteen minutes to talk and catch up on each other's lives, which is usually about ten minutes more than necessary. So we generally fill up the extra time with gratuitous insults.

"I heard you're representing Tony Birch?" Pete asks.

"Proudly. I only wish you had made the arrest; then I'd be positive he was wrongly accused." I know from the discovery that Lieutenant James Lavalle, who works under Pete, has been working the case.

"Lavalle gets all the breaks," Pete says.

"I'll destroy him on the stand. It won't be as easy as cross-examining you, but it will be easy."

"Is anything newsworthy going to come out of this conversation?" Vince asks.

"Here's your headline," Pete says. "'Andy Carpenter's Client Gets Life in Prison and Refuses to Pay Lawyer's Fee.'" Then, to me, he says, "You're going to plead it out, right?"

"The man is innocent."

Pete laughs. "The murder weapon was buried outside his house."

Something about his comment strikes me. "What did you say?"

Another laugh. "You didn't read the discovery? The murder weapon was buried outside his house."

I now have a decision to make: whether to stay and see

the second half or to head home to confirm what I believe. If it was a Giants game, I might stay, but Jacksonville versus Atlanta?

I'm out of here.

If I'm right, this case might just have gotten a whole lot easier.

The team is here at my office for our first case meeting. When Laurie and I arrive, Sam Willis, Edna, Corey Douglas, Willie Miller, and Marcus Clark are already here. As usual, the seats on either side of Marcus are empty. Marcus is an extraordinarily scary guy, and even though he is on our side, it's human nature to steer clear of him.

Laurie doesn't share that particular human nature, so as always she takes a seat next to Marcus. They get along well; she can even understand the grunting sounds he employs instead of actual words. Also here is Eddie Dowd, and it's apparent he has met everyone already.

The other member of our group is in my personal office, and Laurie and I have brought Tara to play with him. That is Simon Garfunkel, Corey Douglas's K-9 partner from their police force days. He and Tara get along great, so we've decided to give them a playdate. It's not necessary for Simon to sit in on the meeting; Corey can update him later on what he needs to know.

"Before we start, I'd like to welcome Eddie Dowd onto the team, replacing Hike Lynch. Hike is moving to South

Carolina and getting married. I, for one, am going to miss his wit. Eddie will assist me on the legal end. So, welcome, Eddie."

"Thanks, Andy," Eddie says. "I'd just like to say that it's a pleasure to pinch-hit for Hike, and as long as I'm in the lineup, I'll give a hundred and ten percent." Apparently Eddie's sports metaphors are not limited to football.

"Thanks, Eddie," I say, and then turn to the group. "Our client is Tony Birch. He is wrongly accused of the murder of one Frankie Zimmer. Zimmer was shot in the back of the head on Bergen Street." I always describe our client as wrongly accused, though quite often, and especially in this case, I have no idea if that's true.

"We have the discovery; I finished going through it for the first time last night. Eddie, if you can hang around after this short meeting, I'd like to take you through part of it. I found something which might be of particular interest.

"Obviously, Laurie, Corey, Marcus, and especially Simon will handle the investigative end. Laurie is up-to-date on where we stand and what we know, so she can update Corey and Marcus. As soon as we've completely digested the discovery, I have no doubt there will be a bunch of people to interview.

"Our client, and the victim, were both members of a gang when they were younger. I'm sure we'll be looking into that area of their lives.

"Sam, you'll obviously handle the tech stuff. For now I'd like you to do a deep dive on the victim, Frankie Zimmer. It would be nice to come up with someone else who might have wanted him dead.

"Willie, no specific assignment yet, but I'm sure we'll need you at some point. Edna . . ." I pause briefly because I can see Edna cringe at what she is about to hear. "Edna . . . you'll continue doing what you do so well. But at this point I can't think of anything specific we need you for right now."

She lets out a deep breath of air, relieved that she has absolutely nothing to do. "I'm on it."

"Good. Of course, when we start filing briefs, there will be some typing involved."

She nods, an acknowledgment that tough times are ahead. "Typing," she says. It has to be the saddest rendition of that word . . . ever.

I field some questions, none of which I have answers for, and we adjourn. Laurie takes Tara home, leaving only Eddie and me. I put the discovery boxes on the table. "You'll need to go through this. But for right now I want you to look at the area I've marked."

He nods and starts to look through it; I've given him the section related to the search warrant and subsequent search of Tony's house. "Something wrong with the warrant?" he asks.

"You tell me."

He starts going through it and says, "They found the gun?" It's not a question he expects an answer to, since we now both know that they found the gun.

After about fifteen minutes, he turns the last page and says, "If there's something unusual here, I don't see it."

"I didn't at first either, and I won't keep you in suspense. The cop saw overturned dirt and dug up the gun. But the warrant was for the interior of the house."

"Wow." He quickly scans the copy of the search warrant again. "Home run."

I share his enthusiasm, though I'd probably consider it a triple. Warrants are drawn with great specificity. The police are obligated to show exactly what they are looking for and, important in this case, where. They were not allowed to dig up the dirt because the warrant was for the interior.

"You think we can win on this?" I ask.

"It's a slam dunk," he says, adding basketball to his repertoire. So far I can keep up; if he starts making cricket or badminton references, I'm going to be lost.

"Can you draft a motion to suppress? I want to get it filed and move quickly before the prosecution has a chance to realize it on their own."

"You got it."

"Edna will type it up." I might as well send him into the fire right away. I know he once dealt with three-hundred-pound offensive linemen intent on taking his head off, but this is the big time. If he can survive asking Edna to do some work, he can handle anything I throw at him.

Washington Park in Newark was upgraded this past summer.

The park had gotten shabby over the years, and the improvement was substantial, and area residents have taken to it quickly. Except in inclement weather, the playgrounds, tennis courts, and ball fields are usually active.

One of the nice things about the park that has obviously remained is that it has a river view, though the banks of the Passaic River will never be confused with the Seine's.

Attendance has slowed down some with the onset of winter, but one feature that remains a popular draw is the dog park. In the renovation it had been landscaped and expanded in size, with new fencing. It's become a social center as well; neighbors come out and can spend hours talking with each other, while their dogs happily socialize on their own.

Dorina Mendoza has a special appreciation for the park. Dorina lives alone, her husband Rodolfo having passed away in April. It is the first time she has ever been by herself in her life, so social interactions are important to her. That is especially true as Christmas is approaching.

Most of her neighbors are couples, and she often feels as if she might be intruding on them when she tries to make a connection. In truth they all like her, but she still feels uncomfortable forcing herself on them.

The dog park has changed that dynamic and presents a double benefit. Her dog, a German shorthaired pointer mix named Chilly, was her husband's dog; Rodolfo primarily cared for him. Now that task has fallen on Dorina, and the problem is that Chilly is a young, large, and active dog and therefore difficult for her to handle.

The park gives Dorina a chance to interact with her neighbors and lets Chilly run himself into exhaustion. It's a win-win.

Some of the people, mostly men, throw tennis balls for the dogs to chase. They don't limit it to their own dogs; that would be impossible. They just throw them and the dogs run after them, en masse. It's semi-organized chaos, but the dogs love it, and the cold weather is not the slightest deterrent.

On this day Dorina had been in the park for over an hour. She had been watching the clouds come in; the weather forecasters on television were predicting freezing rain. Three degrees colder and it could be the first snowstorm of the year.

By this time a lot of people had left, and only a half dozen dogs remained. Tennis balls were still flying, with fewer dogs left to chase them. Chilly, as the largest and most athletic of the bunch, had the most success in running them down.

One of the men threw a tennis ball farther than intended, and it sailed over the five-foot fence. That was not about to stop Chilly, who, without missing a beat, soared over the fence in pursuit of the ball. He chased it for another fifty feet beyond the fence before catching up to it, bringing him down close to the river.

Dorina was immediately concerned; she did not have confidence that Chilly would respond to her calls to come back. He had never been off leash in an area that was not confined. As she and three of the men ran outside and around the fence after him, that concern turned to panic.

Chilly had gotten the ball, then inexplicably dropped it and run toward the river. Dorina was screaming his name, but he was not responding at all. He disappeared over the hill and down toward the riverbank, out of sight of Dorina and the men.

They got to the top of the small hill and looked down. Dorina was relieved to see Chilly digging in a pile of leaves and shrubbery. Intent on what he was doing, he was completely ignoring her pleas to come to her.

Dorina and the men worked their way down the hill. There was no clear path, so they had to navigate it carefully. They beat her down there; she was about thirty feet away when they got to Chilly.

She was twenty feet away when she heard one of the men say, "My God . . ."

She was ten feet away when she saw the decaying body.

I am generally not a big fan of legal technicalities. I say that as a defense attorney, even though we are generally the ones who attempt to take advantage of them. They often inhibit the search for the truth and rarely have anything to do with actual guilt or innocence, so I get why prosecutors look at them with disdain.

But they are some of the few weapons that the defense has, and it is our obligation to take advantage of them when we can.

Today I hope and believe that we can.

In the past three days, Eddie has written, and we've filed, the motion to suppress. It is not a particularly complicated legal position that we are taking, but I was still impressed with Eddie's work on it. It wasn't filled with sports phrases, which was a concern I had. I feared he would say that it was our serve and that it was match point.

The prosecution has responded in writing, and we are in court today so that Judge Baron can hear oral arguments.

Eddie and I sit with Tony Birch at the defense table.

Stan Godfrey and his team are at the prosecution table, and except for court employees and officials, no one else is here. The gallery is empty.

"You think we have a chance at this?" Tony asks.

"Better than fifty-fifty" is my honest reply.

"Good, because I swear that is not my gun. I don't own a gun."

I'm about to respond and tell him that a victory here does not mean the case is over, though it would weaken the prosecution's position substantially. But just then, Judge Baron comes in and gavels the proceedings to order.

Judge Baron is notorious for wanting to move things along quickly, and his view on oral arguments is that they are a waste of time if all they do is repeat what he has already read in the filings.

He informs us of this attitude and then calls on me to state our case. Since the truth is that everything we have to say was in the brief we presented, I'm going to make it short and to the point.

"Thank you, Your Honor. I will not take up much of the court's time, because it's a very simple issue and we covered it fully in our brief. The plain fact is that the gun, regardless of how it got there, was dug up from the dirt outside Mr. Birch's home. The police report is quite clear and definitive as to that point.

"It was outside the very specific area outlined in the search warrant and therefore is clearly tainted and not admissible. For the court to rule otherwise would be to defeat the entire purpose of search warrants, and for that reason we request a ruling that it not be allowed in as evidence, forbidding the prosecution from making any references to it. As you know, the relevant case law is cited in our brief."

"Mr. Godfrey?"

"Your Honor, this is a frivolous defense motion designed to hinder the search for truth. The officer was not there with the intent to violate the terms of the warrant. Nor did he go on a fishing expedition in order to disregard those terms.

"The area where the gun was buried was in plain sight, and the overturned dirt stood out from the rest of the yard. It is really a probable-cause argument. Knowing what he knew about the case, he had reason to believe that the condition of the dirt meant that a crime had been committed; in this case that crime consisted of the concealment and elimination of relevant evidence in a criminal case.

"His investigation of that area, and that area only, was a proper exercise of sound judgment and of him doing his job. If his instinct was ultimately incorrect, then no harm would have been done. If it was correct, as in fact it proved to be, then the search for the truth was advanced. To punish the people of this community by withholding this valuable evidence would run counter to common sense and public safety."

Judge Baron turns to me, so I jump in. "Your Honor, I believe that the public safety is always enhanced by police following the rules. When they do not, as was obviously the case here, then their power is effectively unchecked. I do not have to tell Your Honor that warrants are drawn up with great specificity. That is not happenstance; it is to protect the same public that Mr. Godfrey professes to be concerned about.

"As to Mr. Godfrey's probable-cause argument, I would respectfully say that it makes no sense. There was no urgency to discover an alleged crime being committed, no one was in danger under that dirt. If there was a crime, it had already happened.

"The police could have gone back and gotten an amended warrant, while leaving someone in place to make sure the area was not tampered with. They did not do that, and this court should not let them off the legal hook that their improper actions have left them hanging on."

Godfrey counters with more of the same, but I believe he has a losing position. Judge Baron probably doesn't want to grant our motion to suppress; I'm sure he hates justice-thwarting technicalities much more than I do. But I don't think he has a choice.

I think we are going to win this one, and if we don't, we will have a huge chance of success on an appeal if there is ultimately a conviction. The judge will almost definitely factor that in when considering the matter.

Judge Baron adjourns the hearing to consider the matter, instructing us to come back in one hour. He cautions that he won't necessarily have a decision at that point, but at the very least he'll give us a timetable for that decision to be reached.

Eddie and I walk over to the diner for coffee. I ask him what he thinks, and he says, "I think it was first and goal, and you rammed it in."

Eddie is obviously an optimistic guy, although this

time I agree with him. Regardless, it's a refreshing change from Hike. Hike would have said that we were going to lose and that the judge was going to hold me in contempt for even bringing it up.

Of course, I wouldn't have heard Hike say that because I wouldn't have been crazy enough to have coffee with him.

We get back about fifteen minutes early, and Judge Baron is fifteen minutes late. It all results in a very long half hour.

When he finally takes the bench, he gets right to the point. "There will be a full written opinion forthcoming on the court website, but you should all be aware that I will be granting the motion to suppress."

A slam of the gavel results in a win for us.

A win on a technicality.

But a win. I'll take it.

Eddie Dowd is down at the courthouse filing a motion to dismiss the charges against Tony.

If Godfrey opposes it, as he undoubtedly will, I doubt that Judge Baron will go along with it. It's borderline whether they now have enough to take this to trial, but I think the judge will give them the benefit of the doubt, at least for now.

He just gave us a big win, and my hunch is that he'll lean in the other direction on this one. Eddie agrees, referring to it as a "makeup call," as if the judge is a basketball referee. I should have told Eddie to include in the motion that if the judge rules in our favor, he will make Edna the happiest woman in America.

Of course, we need to operate as if we will lose the motion, so as not to waste time. So, using the list that Tony Birch has written up, we're starting to investigate.

Richie Iurato owns a place called the Basement. It's on Crosby Avenue in Paterson, near where the Tree Tavern Pizza restaurant used to be. I used to get pizza from there all the time; all cheese, none of those ridiculous toppings. Ah, happier times.

I had assumed the Basement was a bar, but it isn't. But I was close. It's a small grocery store that is under a bar; there are steps down from the street to its front door. I have a feeling that more than a few drunken patrons must have descended these steps headfirst.

In most cases I like to just show up to talk to people, rather than call them first. It gives me a chance to see their first reactions to what I'm asking them about and does not give them an opportunity to prepare a narrative or a defense. I'm not sure why, but it's a lot easier to turn down an interview on the phone than in person.

There's one customer in the store, a smallish, elderly woman. A man is helping her get a bottle of dishwashing liquid down from a high shelf. He can't be much more than five foot nine, but he towers over her. He doesn't look at me, but I have a sense that he is aware of every move I make.

He's wearing an apron, so I assume he works here. That's confirmed after he gets the bottle down; they walk to the cashier station and he moves behind the counter and takes her money. He thanks her and she leaves.

"Can I help you?" he asks.

"Are you Richie Iurato?"

"I am." I had expected a "Who wants to know?" kind of response, but didn't get it. This guy is comfortable with who he is.

"My name is Andy Carpenter; I'm an attorney."

Again, no sense of concern on his face. He's obviously not worried about getting sued or arrested. So I add, "Tony Birch's attorney."

"Ah, Tony Birch. My past rears its ugly head." He

actually smiles at the memory, or maybe he is smiling at the knowledge that all of the gang life is safely behind him.

"How so?"

"Tony and I were in a gang together. But I'm sure you already know that." Then, "Damn, that seems so long ago. Maybe because it was."

"Were you and Tony friends, in addition to being in the same gang?"

"No."

He says it with an abruptness and a certainty that surprise me, especially since Tony had listed Iurato as a friend from those days. "Enemies?"

"No." He laughs. "I guess you could say we were colleagues. We sort of had groupings, like cliques, within the gang, and Tony and I were in different ones."

"Did he have any enemies that you know of?"

"Of course. We were in a street gang. Without enemies, street gangs wouldn't exist. They give street gangs a purpose. If you don't have enemies, you create them."

"I'm talking about Tony in particular."

"That was a long time ago."

"Not so long."

"Maybe not in years, but it seems like another lifetime. Look at me; look where I am and what I'm doing. Do I seem threatening to you? But back then, we scared the shit out of people, and other people scared the shit out of us."

"Like Luther?" It's the first time I get any kind of real reaction out of him. It's a slight grimace; maybe fear, or maybe gas. I'm not that good at reaction detecting.

"Like Luther," he says. "I never met the guy, but let's say I was very familiar with his reputation."

"Was Tony scared of Luther?"

"Of course; everybody was scared of Luther."

"Did Luther have any reason to want to hurt Tony?"

"I have no knowledge of that one way or the other, but I can safely say that if he did, Tony wouldn't be around to be your client."

I'm not getting anywhere with him. "Richie, the question on the table is whether you are aware of any people who wanted to do harm to Tony specifically."

For the first time he seems to actually think about the question. "Honestly, I don't know of anyone, but back in those days I wasn't looking at things through a 'Tony prism.' And I also don't know why Tony left."

"What do you mean?"

"Look, I wasn't really on the inside; I was more of a hanger-on. I didn't participate in any decisions, you know? Tony was in what you would call our leadership group; he was exposed to different pressures."

"Understood."

"But I remember that all of a sudden Tony wasn't there anymore. I didn't care much either way, but I remember wondering what happened."

"Did you ask?"

"Yeah. I asked a couple of people. One of them, now that I think of it, was Frankie Zimmer."

"What did he say?"

Richie laughs. "That it was none of my business. I think it was about then that I decided to become a grocery tycoon."

"You have any guess as to what might have happened?"

"Not really, other than he could have pissed off the wrong people."

"Who might that have been?"

"Sorry. I have no idea." A little bell rings above the door, as a customer comes in. "Anything else I can help you with?"

I reach down below the counter. "I'll take these Peanut M&M's."

You're wanted at the courthouse at two P.M.," Laurie says.

It's on a message on my cell phone that I retrieve when I leave the Basement. I can hardly hear it because the connection isn't great, and I'm chomping on my Peanut M&M's.

I love Peanut M&M's. I used to think I preferred the blue ones, but then Laurie did a blind taste test on me, which demonstrated I couldn't tell the difference. I don't know why she does things like that to me; next she'll tell me there's no such thing as the tooth fairy.

I call Laurie back to confirm that I received the message and to ask if she knows what it's about.

"No, but they were pretty insistent. You are to go straight to Judge Baron's chambers when you get there."

I'm a little worried by this. I suppose the purpose of the meeting could be to announce the dropping of the charges, but that doesn't seem likely. That could be done in a phone call and a statement from the court. Certainly there would be no necessity for an in-person meeting.

My fear is that it could be Judge Baron's changing his

mind about the motion to suppress. He did announce it in open court, so reversing himself would be embarrassing, but nothing he could not handle. Ominously, the granting of our motion has not yet made it to the court's official website.

The third possibility is that there is a new development, perhaps some additional evidence has been uncovered. But that is also unlikely; Judge Baron wouldn't be involved in conveying that news. It would come from Godfrey's office as additional discovery.

I have time to grab lunch before the meeting time, so that's what I do. I debate whether to call Eddie and tell him to meet me at the courthouse, but decide against it. My guess is that my role in this meeting is to listen, not to talk, and I don't need backup for that.

When I get there, Godfrey is waiting outside the judge's chambers. After we insincerely exchange "How are you?" I ask him if he knows why we are here.

"I do. Sorry, but I'm not at liberty to say. The judge wants to handle this."

Of the three possibilities, two have just dropped out of the running; Godfrey is too obviously relishing what is about to happen. The judge is changing his mind about the motion to suppress, even though it was the correct ruling. I am going to win this on appeal if I have to go all the way to the Supreme Court.

The clerk comes out to tell us that the judge is waiting for us, so we go in. I am getting angrier with each step; this is a travesty of justice.

When we arrive, I see a court reporter is there to record everything that is said. It's another bad sign.

"Okay, I'll get right to the point," Judge Baron says after we're seated. "Mr. Godfrey knows some but not all of what I am going to say, but I wanted both sides represented when I say it."

"There have been two new developments in the case. A Mr."—he looks at his notes—"Raymond Hackett . . . was found deceased in a Newark park earlier this week. He was shot from a short distance, one bullet in the back of the head. The body was apparently partially obscured by shrubbery and therefore was not quickly discovered. The estimate is that he had been dead for at least two weeks, possibly longer."

He pauses, but I know where this is going. "Ballistics show that the murder weapon was the same as the one used to kill Mr. Zimmer. I should also tell you that I have been informed as to what seems to be a credible connection between Mr. Birch and Mr. Hackett."

I could start to argue this now; my contention is that a second murder doesn't necessarily tie this to Tony Birch and doesn't make the tainted search any cleaner. But my sense is that I should wait to see where Judge Baron is going with this.

"Mr. Godfrey has subsequently brought something to the attention of the court in a newly filed brief. Mr. Carpenter, it is obviously your right to file a rebuttal, but I felt that since I gave an informal ruling on your motion to suppress, it is proper and fair that we discuss this first.

"Mr. Godfrey has directed me to a Supreme Court case; are you familiar with *Nix versus Williams*?"

"No," I say. I leave out that the only Nicks I know is

Stevie. Oh, and Hakeem, who used to be a wide receiver for the Giants.

"I have a copy of the opinion for you. But basically it created an inevitable discovery exception to the exclusionary rule. The prosecution has to credibly demonstrate that even had they not discovered the weapon improperly, they would have done so eventually and inevitably through acceptable means.

"Mr. Godfrey has provided, as part of his brief, eleven examples in the past two years when the police department has sought and been granted second and third warrants to search the outside of a property when the interior search did not turn up the materials they were seeking.

"It seems completely credible that after seeing the overturned dirt, had they not searched the area in the moment, they would in fact have done so later under an amended warrant. I am therefore convinced that this situation satisfies the *Nix* requirements, especially in light of the second murder with that gun. There is also a public safety issue at play, though I don't need to get to that to alter my ruling. *Nix* provides ample justification."

"So you've made your decision?" I ask, though I obviously know the answer.

"Pending your written arguments; you are entitled to that opportunity. But in light of the fact that I am changing my original oral ruling, something I am ordinarily loathe to do, I wanted to give you notice as to my reasoning. If you cannot successfully argue that *Nix* does not apply, your arguments will be futile."

"This was a fun meeting," I say. "Let's do this again real soon."

I leave the meeting and head home. Eddie and I will file a rebuttal brief, but it will go nowhere. Every word out of Judge Baron's mouth guaranteed that our arguments are not going to prevail; he came right out and said it.

But that wasn't the worst thing he said.

The worst thing he said was there "seems to be a credible connection between Mr. Birch and Mr. Hackett."

hate to speak ill of the dead, but society will not miss Frankie Zimmer," Sam says.

Sam has come over to the house to give his initial report. He could have called or sent it in writing, but Sam is fond of eating, and he knows we always have a lot of food in the house. I can't remember the last report Sam gave when he wasn't chewing; this time he is chomping on Laurie's French toast.

"I've gone through all of his records, police files, court documents, juvenile records, and publicly available stuff," he says.

I don't ask him how he accessed the stuff that wasn't publicly available because I have no desire to know. Chances are I wouldn't understand it anyway. The truth is that the vast majority of information that Sam gets for me by questionable means are materials we could eventually get legally, but that process is always much slower, and that inhibits our investigation. It also tips the prosecution off on what we're looking for. Later, if we want to introduce any of it in court, we subpoena it legally.

Sam continues, "I started when he was fifteen, around

the time of his first arrest. He and two buddies mugged a guy."

"Was Tony Birch one of the buddies?"

"No. Zimmer's glorious history goes on from there; he's been arrested twenty-one times, charged nine times, and actually gone to jail four times. He spent a total of six and a half of his miserable thirty-two-year life behind bars. And it could have been more."

"What does that mean?"

"He was an informant for the police, and he used it to accumulate get-out-of-jail-free cards. But the big one was when they nailed him on a home robbery. He apparently thought the house was empty, but a woman inconveniently turned out to be home. He scared the shit out of her, grabbed some stuff, and ran. The police caught him within an hour; this is not a guy with Richard Kimble level skills."

"And he got off?"

Sam nods. "By testifying against Tony Birch. He was one of the witnesses who sent Birch away."

This is not news; we knew that Zimmer testified against Tony. If anything, Zimmer's doing it as a way to get out of his own situation makes me feel a bit better. It means he had a reason to lie, which tends to increase the credibility of Tony's claim of innocence to the manslaughter for which he was imprisoned.

"What about gang activity?" I ask.

"It was an open secret. They called themselves the Fulton Street Boyz."

"Did you find anything in these records about Luther and the Blood Dragons?"

"No. You want me to look into that?"

"Yes, but first I want you to check out a guy named Raymond Hackett."

"That sounds familiar," Sam says. "Who is he?"

"I don't have any information on him except for the fact that he was murdered a few weeks ago. I'm sure it will be in the media later today."

"Uh-oh. I need to check something." Sam starts looking through the papers he brought with him. Then, "That's why his name sounded familiar."

"Why?" I start going into my bad-news cringe.

"Remember I told you that Zimmer wasn't the only one to testify against Tony Birch? Raymond Hackett did as well."

The breaking news of Hackett's murder has elevated Birch's case in media-land.

What was an isolated murder has now become much more, and a thirsty media can even smell a possible serial killer. There isn't much that excites them more than that.

Unfortunately, if the media thinks a story is important, the public will soon follow. And even more unfortunately, that public will make up the jury pool. The media will, of course, use the word *alleged* when talking about Tony's potential guilt, but there has never been a more invisible and easily overlooked word than *alleged.*

"Do you have a chance to keep out the gun?" Laurie asks.

"Zero. Eddie's drafted a brief, but it's us on one side, and the Supreme Court on the other. As Eddie would put it, that's game, set, and match."

"So we have two murders, motives for both, and the murder weapon buried in Tony's backyard."

"When you put it like that it doesn't sound that great."

She laughs. "You have another way to put it?"

"Not so far."

"You think he did them?"

"Very possibly, but also very possibly not."

"Tell me the not part, Andy. I'd like something to grab on to." Laurie still looks at things through the eyes of a cop, so she wants our clients to be innocent as much as or more than I do.

"It's not much, but here goes. There are some things that don't make sense to me. Tony gets out of jail, turns his life around, builds a business, and then gets his revenge? And back-to-back murders like that, using the identical MO? If he had the patience to wait all those years, he could have spread them out. This way it's like shining a light on himself. Tony seems smarter than that."

"Anything else?" she asks, obviously not convinced.

I nod. "The gun. If he's guilty, then he shot Hackett and kept the gun because he was going to need it again. Then he shot Zimmer on Bergen Street and brought the gun home with him. Why not dispose of it?"

"Where?"

"Anywhere. As long as he wiped his prints off, he could have left it on the steps of the police department. What's the difference where he left it? It couldn't be tied to him. In fact, the only way to tie the gun to him would be to do exactly what he did. Once again, I think Tony is smarter than that. I think Sebastian is smarter than that."

"Maybe he was going to use the gun again and he was hiding it."

"Hide it in dirt?"

"Maybe the handkerchief was there to protect it."

"Maybe," I say. "Or maybe not."

"Okay. So what's next, boss?"

"You and your team should try and find as many members of the gang Tony was in, the Fulton Street Boyz. Whatever is going on goes back to those days. We're looking to find out who had grudges against Zimmer and Hackett, but more importantly, we want to know who had reason for revenge against Tony."

"Because they set him up."

"Right. The real murderer, if it's not Tony, did not need to set him up. These two hits could have been done without a trace; it wasn't necessary to make Tony the fall guy. I don't know if the real killer was after all three, or if Zimmer and Hackett were just means to an end."

"What are you going to do?"

"Talk to my client. He's been holding something back."

I head down to the jail to talk to Tony; I'm going to be tough with him, and he is either going to respond, or he's going to spend the rest of his life in jail.

Before he is even fully seated, I say, "Tell me about Raymond Hackett."

"He was in the gang. We were friends; I thought we had each other's back."

"But you didn't?"

"He had my back and then he stabbed me in it. He testified against me, along with Zimmer."

"Why?"

Tony shakes his head. "I don't know. I could never figure it out. Maybe you could ask him that."

"Or maybe not. He's dead. Shot in the back of his head, like Zimmer."

"Damn. What the hell is going on?" Before I have a

chance to answer, he says, "Hey, doesn't that help our case? I'm in here. How could I have killed him?"

"He's been dead for a while; they just found the body. You weren't in here when he got hit."

The disappointment on Tony's face is evident; he thought this might have gotten him off the hook. I'm about to tell him that the hook is alive and well, and he's hanging on it.

"Hackett was shot with the same gun. And that gun is now going to be admissible."

"No . . . I thought we won that?"

"The Supreme Court disagreed. Why did you leave the gang?"

"What? . . . I . . . had had enough. I wanted to get out of that world."

"Bullshit."

"Come on, I—"

I interrupt, "The next words that come out of your mouth better provide the answer to my question." I don't threaten that I'll quit the case; I am positive he is getting that message without my directly stating it.

He nods; it's a concession, a sign of defeat. "Something happened. Something awful."

"Tell me all of it."

"There were four of us; we were sort of the leaders. It was me, Zimmer, Hackett, and TJ Richardson. We had sort of separated ourselves from the others; a gang within a gang. Not officially, but we got the more important assignments."

"From Luther?"

"Yeah, but still not directly. They came to us from his guy, the one we usually dealt with. I mentioned him to you before; his name was Russell Estrada.

"But I'm sure Luther was calling the shots. One day we got a job to do from Estrada; it was a collection. Nothing out of the ordinary; this stuff happened all the time. Somebody hadn't been paying up, and Luther wanted to send a message. We were the messengers."

"Who was the guy?"

"His name was Josh Winkler, or Winkle, or something like that. I think he was an advertising executive. Rich guy who was trying to stay rich by not paying his drug bills."

"You were part of the collection job?"

"No. We used to divide up the assignments. There was no need for everybody to go everywhere. This job went to TJ Richardson. It was a one-man job, but Zimmer went as backup, just to observe. We always had a backup in case something went wrong. Usually a guy like that, you just have to scare him, at least the first time."

"Did something go wrong?"

"Yeah. Very wrong. The guy was carrying, and he pulled the gun on TJ. There was shooting coming from both sides. I think they both were hiding behind cars, shooting at each other. TJ . . . one of his bullets hit a kid . . . eight years old. She died instantly." Tony shakes his head at the memory. "Eight years old."

"Was Zimmer involved, since he was a backup?"

"I don't think so; if he was, it never came out. It went down as if TJ was trying to mug this Winkler guy, and he was defending himself."

"You definitely weren't there?"

"No, but I could have been; that's the point. It could have been me that got the job, and when the guy pulled a gun, I would have pulled mine and started shooting. Just like TJ did. And I could have been the one to kill that kid. I was lucky . . . TJ wasn't. And that poor kid definitely wasn't."

Another pause; it's as if he is reliving that time in his mind. "That's why I got out."

"What happened to TJ?"

"The cops nailed him and he got forty years. He was knifed to death in a prison fight a year later."

"Some people would say he got what was coming to him."

Tony nods. "Yeah. And right now there are people saying that about me."

I'm finding that I'm starting to like Tony, though I have to admit that my history includes liking some people that I subsequently learned were murderers. That could easily happen here.

"I'm going to need to get into your house," I say.

He doesn't ask why, which surprises me. Maybe he's starting to trust me and understand that he has to depend on me.

"Okay. I'll call Chuck and tell him to drop off a key to the house at your office. They're pretty good about letting me make phone calls."

"Who's Chuck?"

"Chuck Holmes. He works for me down at the shop. He's maybe a little slower than most. But he's a good worker and loyal." Then, "Actually, it's going to be your shop, so he really works for you."

The image of me owning an auto service shop is so ridiculous that I can't help smiling. "I don't think so." I stand up. "But have him drop it off as soon as he can. I'll get back to you."

As I near the door, he asks, "How's Zoey?"

"She's adorable. She's got plenty of friends she can play with." I don't mention that Willie's assessment is that she doesn't seem happy.

"Does she miss me?" He smiles a sad smile.

"I'm sure she does. I'll ask her."

That Stan Godfrey hasn't called me sums up the situation pretty well.

The government is almost always inclined to accept a plea bargain, albeit on their terms. Trials are expensive, labor-intensive, and time-consuming. If prosecutors can get a win without going through any of that, and without risking a defeat, they are happy to claim victory and move on to the next case.

Godfrey obviously has no interest in making a deal. That says two things. One is that he doesn't see the possibility of losing, so the risk element is not a factor. Two is that the elements of these crimes, the lying in wait and shooting in the back of the head, are so onerous that the government would insist on such a long prison term that there would be no reason for the defense to accept a deal.

Maybe, if I went to him, we could get a forty-year sentence rather than life. But Tony would never go for that, nor should he. Forty years in state prison is not something you accept without a fight. And if he's innocent, obviously a big if, then spending that many years behind bars would be uniquely cruel and awful.

I go back to the office to see if more discovery documents have arrived. They have, along with a notice that Essex County, where Hackett's body was found, has agreed to have his trial be handled in Passaic County.

What that means is that our trial will be for both murders, which isn't terribly upsetting. Whoever did one did the other; we just have to demonstrate that it wasn't Tony. On one level it's even a plus; if we can exonerate him on either one of the charges, the other one will crumble as well.

Combining the two murders into one trial is yet another example of Godfrey's confidence. Often in a situation like this they would prefer to try one charge at a time. If they try them simultaneously and happen to lose, then jeopardy attaches and they never get another chance. If only one charge is tried, then a loss still leaves the prosecution with another bite at the apple.

Godfrey is content to eat the entire apple at one sitting.

I start to go through the discovery on the Hackett shooting, which is fairly sparse. The police do not know much; there were no witnesses to the crime. They are sure that the murder took place where the body was found, based on the blood and that they found a shell casing. Their theory is that branches were thrown on top of the body to at least partially conceal it.

What they don't have an explanation for, at least in these documents, is what Hackett was doing there. This was not the Atlantic City boardwalk; the Newark bank of the Passaic River is not a place one goes to for a stroll. And if for some bizarre reason Hackett was out for such a stroll, how would the killer have known to have been there, concealed and ready to shoot?

My obvious guess is that the killer brought Hackett there, probably at gunpoint, and then shot him. It's interesting that Hackett's body was partially concealed, but Zimmer was murdered on a downtown street. I'm sure the prosecution will claim that it was done that way because Hackett was killed first, and Tony wanted to make sure he would have the time and opportunity to kill Zimmer.

I also find it somewhat interesting that Hackett was shot in the back of the head. If the killer brought him there at gunpoint, there would have been no reason to shoot from behind, or for that matter in the back of the head. Both obviously could have happened, but it almost seems like an attempt to create the same MO that would subsequently be used in the Zimmer killing.

I'm getting ready to leave when there is a knock on the door. I have no idea who it is; there is no doorman stationed in the fruit stand below to call up and announce visitors.

"Come in," I call out, which is a line I cleverly use to prevent my having to get up.

The door opens and a guy is standing there, literally in grease-stained overalls. I'm guessing he's the mechanic who works for Tony, and not a Supreme Court justice. "Chuck?"

"Yes, sir. I didn't know anyone was in; I was just dropping off the key to Tony's . . . Mr. Birch's . . . house."

"Great." I stand and hold out my hand. "I'm Andy Carpenter."

He shakes my hand weakly; fortunately it's not greasy like his clothing. "Chuck . . . Holmes." The guy is obviously nervous. Tony also described him as slightly slow, and that is coming across as well.

"You work with Tony?"

He smiles sort of an embarrassed smile; this is not someone who is comfortable in anything resembling social situations. "I work *for* him," he says, emphasis on the *for*. Then, "But he's my friend."

Chuck is just standing there, next to the sofa, making no effort to leave, so I'm forced into "make conversation" mode. It is not my favorite mode; "cherry pie á la" is my favorite mode. "How long have you known him?"

He pauses to think about his answer; he's more concerned with accuracy than I am at the moment. "Seven months, ever since he hired me."

"Okay, well, thanks for coming by and bringing this." I hold up the key to remind him what he brought.

"No problem. Anything Mr. Tony needs."

He's still standing there. "Sorry, but I need to get back to work." I point to my desk, as a way of showing him where my work is. It feels like this meeting has lasted a couple of weeks.

He gets the hint and leaves. I go to the window to make sure he's gone and across the street before I leave myself. I do not want to run into him and have another scintillating conversation.

I see him and watch him reach the end of the block. The coast is therefore clear; I'm out of here.

She's gone, Andy. Zoey's gone."

The clock says five forty-five in the morning, and even though the phone just woke me up, Willie's panicked voice sounds like he's been up for a while.

"What happened, Willie?"

"Sondra was going outside to get the paper. She didn't even realize that Zoey was nearby, but when she opened the door, Zoey got out. She just took off running. By the time Sondra called me downstairs, she was long out of sight."

"Okay. We need to drive around your neighborhood. Sondra should stay home in case she comes back."

"I'm in the car now; I haven't seen any sign of her."

"I'll be there as soon as I can."

For anyone who loves dogs, this is a potential nightmare. The idea of losing a dog in one's care is horrifying and can lead to a permanent guilt. For Willie and for me, this situation is even worse because we were responsible for Zoey on behalf of someone else.

I quickly get dressed, telling Laurie what is going on as I do so. I bring Tara with me; if we find Zoey, she might be afraid and unwilling to get in the car. Tara's presence might overcome that.

Willie lives about ten minutes from us, so in case Zoey happened to run in this direction, I keep my eyes alert the entire time to see her. As I get closer to Willie's house, when I see people on the street, I stop and ask if they've seen any sign of a dog off leash. No one says that they have.

I call Willie and we loosely divide up the search area. This is not scientific, and it doesn't matter if we overlap. "Let's call each other immediately if one of us sees her," I say.

"Right. Andy, Sondra is so upset." I can hear the pain in Willie's voice.

"It's not her fault, Willie. It could happen to anyone."

"That's what I told her, but it didn't help."

"Did Zoey have a tag on her with your name and number?" I ask.

"Of course."

"Then she'll turn up."

The Passaic County Animal Shelter will open at 8:00 A.M. I make a mental note to call Fred Brandenberger, who runs it. Fred and I know each other well; we rescue a lot of dogs from that shelter. I will alert Fred that Zoey is missing, and I'll describe her. That way if someone brings her there, he'll know to call me and Willie.

My route takes me through a forty-square-block area, and after a while I expand it to eighty blocks. Zoey is a fairly young, active dog; she could have traveled far by now. The scary thing is that I'm driving near Route 46, and at this hour cars are traveling quite fast. I can only hope that Zoey doesn't venture near there.

Willie and I drive around for four hours, occasionally checking in with each other by phone. We finally give up; by now Zoey could be anywhere.

This is already as bad a day as I have had in a long time.

We will soon have to investigate Luther and the Blood Dragons.

I don't have a particular reason to think Luther is involved in the Zimmer or Hackett killings, but when one is trying to identify potential murder suspects, it's always best to consider actual murderers. And Luther, according to everyone I talk to, checks that box.

By Tony's account, four guys were in the small unit within the Fulton Street gang that were ranked higher than the others. Those were the four that got the order from Luther, though the actual contact was Russell Estrada, to collect from the ad executive. TJ Richardson drew the assignment, and it blew up in his face. And it left a little girl dead on the street.

The others in the group of four haven't done much better. Zimmer and Hackett were themselves murdered, and Tony is sitting in jail facing life in prison for crimes he swears he did not commit.

It's possible, even quite probable, that the incident that killed the little girl has nothing to do with the current case. But the four no doubt drew other assignments from

Luther, and maybe the answer lies in one of them. By all accounts, Luther and his gang are scary guys that have killed people in the past, so that makes them interesting to me as potential villains in our case.

Right now I'm keeping my focus on the episode that drove Tony out of the gang, which is why I'm at Grantham and Winkler, an ad agency on Thirty-second Street between Lexington and Third Avenue in Manhattan.

I've had Sam do some quick research on Josh Winkler, starting by confirming that he was the man who was involved in the incident during which TJ Richardson accidentally shot the little girl. Winkler never faced any charges for what happened; he had a license to carry the gun and was clearly acting in self-defense. It also was not his gun that fired the fatal shot.

Winkler is a cofounder and partner in the agency. According to Sam, they are basically a creative shop, and highly thought of, which is why they have been able to resist the consolidation of the advertising industry into a few mega-agencies. They subcontract to one of those agencies to do their media placement, while keeping their focus on creating campaigns.

When I called him, Winkler was not anxious, as expected, to talk to me and relive what must have been a stressful time. I turned on the understanding and compassionate side of Andy Carpenter and threatened that if he didn't meet with me, I would force him to testify publicly and make sure the press was all over the story.

So here I am.

Grantham and Winkler occupies the top two floors of a twelve-story building. Buildings in New York are often referred to as prewar or postwar, depending on their age. The *war* in question is World War II, but I think this building is pre–War of 1812.

The elevator is the ancient kind where a metal gate closes along with the door itself. Not only could I sing an entire Broadway show tune in the time it takes me to get to the twelfth floor . . . I could compose one. But since I am always one to look at the bright side, this is probably the only elevator in New York that doesn't play Christmas music.

The elevator door finally opens and I step off onto another planet entirely. Grantham and Winkler is stunningly modern; it looks like it was redone about an hour ago. It is completely incongruous to the building it's in; it's jarring, and maybe that's the reaction they are hoping for.

Within five minutes of my telling the receptionist who I am, she leads me back to Winkler's office. On the way I pass posters of ad campaigns, many of which are familiar to me. They sell movies, and toothpaste, and cameras, and computers, and pretty much everything else.

Winkler is sitting at his desk when the receptionist lets me in. For some reason I expected someone younger; he's probably in his midfifties. He looks up but does not stand and does not offer a handshake. Instead he just points to the chair across from his desk. "Take a seat."

I'm not feeling loved.

"What do you want to know?"

"The night the shooting happened, when the girl was killed, you were acting in self-defense?"

"That's right. A guy came at me with a gun."

"Why?"

"How do I know? He wasn't a pissed-off client, that much I can tell you. He probably wanted to rob me; I wasn't about to wait to find out."

"Why were you carrying a gun?"

"I have a license and I keep it for protection. That night proved it was necessary."

"So he wanted money?"

He nods. "That's my best guess."

"Could it be that he was there to collect money that you owed to Luther?"

I've clearly struck a nerve, which would be good news if I was in the nerve-striking business. Unfortunately I'm currently in the information-gathering business, and I'm no longer expecting to get any from this interview.

Finally he says, "I don't know what you're talking about, or who that Luther guy is."

"I can help you with that. He's the guy whose people were selling you drugs."

"This conversation is over," he says, as much afraid as defiant.

"Look, I'm not trying to cause you problems. I don't care if you took drugs or not, or if you paid for them or not. Something that happened that night may have been the catalyst to get three other people killed, and one is facing life in prison. I'm trying to understand what that could be."

He thinks for a while, as if deciding whether to talk some more. Finally he says, "It was a rough time in my life. I did some stupid things, and I dealt with some pretty bad people. But I ultimately paid my debts, and I put all of it behind me."

He takes a deep breath. "And I haven't dealt with those people again in all the years since. Nor have I taken any drugs in all that time. So I can't give you what you're looking for because I just don't know anything about it."

"How long since you've seen Luther?"

"I only saw him once, when we made our arrangements. After that I dealt with his people. And after that night we settled up, and I never saw them again. Which is exactly how I like it."

I stand up. "Okay, hopefully you won't hear from me again either."

"I hope not. None of this came out back then, and I don't want it to come out now."

I just nod. I can't promise it won't come out because I don't yet know if I'll need this information to help my client.

As I'm leaving, he says, "I will tell you this: those are not people you want to have as an enemy."

I just nod, since I knew that already. After the four-hour elevator ride down to street level, I call Willie to see if there's any news about Zoey. I'm sure there isn't; if there was, he would have called me.

"She's nowhere, Andy. I keep driving around, and so does Sondra. I posted signs all over offering a reward, but nobody has called."

"I'll take a run through the area on the way home. You never know."

It's hard to believe, but Christmas Day snuck up on me.

I think it's because in Laurie's world, in which I happen to be an inhabitant, Christmas isn't actually a day. It's a four-month season of lights, decorations, a tree, and the ever-present music. If they don't use relentless Christmas music in POW camps to make prisoners confess, they're missing out on a sure thing.

But all of a sudden the day is here, and the reason I know that is because Laurie told me last night that it was Christmas Eve. From there it's a simple matter of deduction, and I am a master at deduction.

Laurie and I had decided that we wouldn't give each other gifts this year; our cruise was going to count as our gift to each other. I'm not crazy enough to have actually gone along with that, so I secretly bought her a necklace.

On the rare occasions that I buy jewelry for Laurie, I'm not really getting something for her to keep and wear. It's really a place setter, so she'll be able to return it and get something she likes. It's not that I have bad taste in jewelry; I don't have any taste in it at all. I don't have a clue.

So the drill is that I give it to her and she pretends to

like it. I spend the next couple of hours encouraging her to exchange it, and she finally agrees to go down to the store and look. She swears that she will keep the original, and that she's just looking to satisfy me. Then she goes there, exchanges it, and gets something she actually likes. Next occasion it's rinse, buy, return, repeat.

Ricky is easy to buy for, at least for me, because I don't do the buying. Laurie takes care of it; my only input is to beg her not to get anything that requires assembly. This year she went along with that, and Ricky seems happy with his gifts.

Christmas is a quiet day for us. We eat in the early afternoon and just hang out. There are always five good NBA games on; it's not Thanksgiving Day football, but it's pretty good.

A pall is hovering over us since Zoey is still missing. I'm becoming pessimistic about ever finding her, while Laurie claims at least to be remaining positive. I'm going to have to tell Tony what happened. I owe him that, but I absolutely dread it.

Unfortunately, murder cases aren't holiday sensitive, so I can't waste an entire day without at least thinking about legal and investigative strategy. So with the televised games as background noise, I go through the discovery again. I'll do this at least a dozen times, until everything about the case becomes embedded in my brain.

I don't expect a revelation and I don't get one. Nothing has changed; there's not a shred in here that is exculpatory for Tony. Since I have nothing to base a defense on, it's a little tough to plan a defense strategy, but I have to at least start the process.

I told Josh Winkler that something about the shooting incident years ago set off a chain reaction that has gotten us where we are today. The truth is that I have no idea if I was right about that; I was just saying it to get a reaction. I got a reaction, but it didn't lead me anywhere.

The task ahead of us is daunting. Two ex–gang guys, both with extensive criminal records, have been killed, years after their gang activity was over. Just by nature of their history, Zimmer and Hackett must have associated with many dangerous people. I have no way of knowing who those people are, or whether they had a reason to kill them.

But all we can do is re-create their recent lives as best we can. I'll put Laurie and the K Team on that starting tomorrow, and I'll pitch in as well.

If we're operating under the assumption that Tony is innocent—and there is no other way we can operate—then somebody is framing him. The murder weapon didn't bury itself in his yard. Tony would make an obvious patsy; it was well-known that Hackett and Zimmer testified against him and put him in prison. It would be a no-brainer to credibly paint him as having a motive to exact revenge.

Tony almost certainly made other enemies that he might not even be aware of. TJ Richardson was sent to collect money from Josh Winkler, at the behest of Luther and the Blood Dragons. No doubt there were many similar assignments, some of which Tony, Zimmer, and Hackett carried out. Any of those jobs could have resulted in the targeted people coming back for their own revenge.

Then there is Luther himself, though I consider it less

likely. I've never dealt with him, but his reputation is such that if he had a beef with Tony, he would just send his people to kill him. Frame-ups don't seem like his style. But we certainly cannot eliminate him as a possibility.

Then there are the people that Tony must have encountered while in prison. Few of them walked around with halos; they were by definition criminals, and in many or most cases, violent ones. Tony could easily have pissed off some of them.

So there are seemingly endless possibilities, with little time to sort through them.

Merry Christmas.

I'm going to take Tara and Sebastian for a walk.

The sound of my cell phone ringing is jarring.

Actually, *ringing* isn't the correct term. My phone plays "The Godfather" music; I'm not sure what the psychological implications of that might be. But walking in a deathly quiet Eastside Park on Christmas night with Tara and Sebastian, it sounds like a full orchestra is playing it.

Caller ID tells me that it's Laurie, which instantly worries me that something is going wrong at home. Since I left there just twenty minutes ago, that seems unlikely. It might have something to do with our case.

All this goes through my mind in the four or five seconds it takes me to press the button and say, "Hello?"

"There's a third murder connected to the gun," she says.

"Please tell me it happened while Tony has been in jail." I then immediately realize what a stupid comment that was. The gun has been in police custody since it was found at his house, so it couldn't have been used in a homicide since.

"Sorry. It happened six weeks ago in Scranton, Pennsylvania. They just made the discovery now through NIBIN.

Corey found out about it through a connection in the Department."

"I'm heading home." Might as well talk it out in person, rather than standing in the park trying to balance holding a phone and two leashes.

I already understand the basics of what happened. NIBIN is the National Integrated Ballistic Information Network, and its basic function is to share ballistics information between states. Obviously the Paterson cops put the specs on the gun that killed Zimmer and Hackett into the system, and it kicked out this other murder.

When I get home, Laurie is waiting with a couple of glasses of wine, and we sit in the den. The NBA game is still on the television, but I mute the sound. I could turn it off entirely, but it's Lakers-Celtics, and I do have my priorities.

"The victim is a guy named Terry Banner," she says. "He's a TV newscaster for a local Scranton station."

"The name sounds familiar."

She nods. "It did to me also, so I googled him and found out why. He used to be on Channel Five in New York. He did a short segment three times a week, mostly bringing out otherwise obscure stories that his audience should be outraged about."

"Right. I remember now. Any connection to Tony?"

"None that I saw. Might be a good idea to put Sam on it."

"Good idea." I call Sam and tell him all that we know. "I need to know if there's a connection to Tony Birch."

"I'll call you back." He hangs up.

Having accomplished that, I turn back to Laurie. "How was he killed?"

"Shot in the back of the head coming home late at night. According to reports, he was in his garage."

"Did anyone hear the shot? Do they know the time that it happened?"

"I don't know; the reports don't say."

"This could turn out to be good news, though clearly not for Terry Banner or a member of the Banner family."

"How so?"

"If Tony has an alibi, if he was addressing a meeting of the Daughters of the American Revolution at the time the killing took place, then it basically gets him off the hook on all three homicides. It's a stretch for the prosecution to claim that the gun is being passed from murderer to murderer."

"What if he has no alibi? What if he spent the night at home, without throwing a party or ordering a pizza?"

"Then as far as our case goes, it's a nonevent. The Banner death could not be included in our trial, nor can evidence about the gun being used, unless there is direct evidence tying Tony to it. It's in a different jurisdiction. We can bring it in if it benefits us, but the prosecution can't use it unless we open that door."

"Good."

"If they can't tie Tony to Banner, then it will interesting to see what Godfrey does with this."

"What do you mean?" she asks.

"I'm interested in whether or not he turns it over in discovery, because if it doesn't implicate Tony, then it's exculpatory."

Eventually we stop talking about this, much to the relief of both of us. It's a couple of hours later, as we're getting into bed, that the phone rings. At least this time it's the landline, and it's just a regular old-fashioned ring, not *The Godfather* music. A nighttime ringing phone sounds much less ominous in a bedroom than in Eastside Park.

"I didn't wake you, did I?" Sam asks.

"No. Did you find out anything?"

"I did. Back around the time that Tony killed the guy in the fight, Banner did a televised piece on street violence, and how police in the metropolitan area weren't doing enough to keep it under control. Like all of his pieces, it was designed to piss people off."

"Uh-oh." I have this sinking feeling, like there's an anvil in my stomach.

"He used Tony and his situation with that manslaughter case to make his point."

Will this Christmas Day ever be over?

Corey's finding out about Terry Banner's murder through a contact didn't give us much of a head start.

We would have found out about it today anyway, not through brilliant detective work, but rather by turning on the television. It's being treated here as a big story for two reasons.

One is that Banner was once a member of the local media, so it hits home. Somehow the story of his death, when first reported locally in Scranton, slipped under the New York media radar. They are making up for it now, and my sense is that he wasn't well liked by his press colleagues, but that could be me reading too much into the coverage.

The other reason it's a big story is that whoever leaked it . . . and I'm looking at you, Godfrey . . . also leaked that the same gun was used as in the Zimmer and Hackett killings. This can be damaging to our case, which is why Godfrey leaked it.

The New York media has also uncovered that Banner had run a piece when he was in New York using Tony as a whipping boy for street violence. The implication is obvious: if Tony has a grudge against you, you wind up with a bullet in the back of your head.

I don't see any way that the Banner murder can come into play in our trial. Judge Baron would almost definitely see it as more prejudicial than probative. That Banner ran a negative media piece on Tony certainly has no place in our courtroom; how can anyone possibly assume that Tony was angry about it or wanted revenge? How could they even prove he knew about it?

But Godfrey, if he was in fact the leaker, has effectively gotten it in front of the jury by doing this end around. The jury will be a group of private citizens, and most of those citizens will be exposed to a media story of this magnitude.

Eddie is filing a brief in protest, demanding that the charges be dropped for this grievous example of prosecutorial misconduct. It will fail and at best elicit a modest reprimand from the judge, which Godfrey will shrug off, after he denies being the leaker in the first place.

So it's back to the jail to find out what Tony can add to the story and, most important, whether he can prove that he was not in Scranton on the night of the murder.

When he's finally brought in, I start off by telling him that Terry Banner is dead.

He looks either genuinely puzzled or fake puzzled. "Who is that?"

"He's a newscaster who did a negative story on you after the incident which sent you to prison the first time."

"Not ringing a bell."

"You don't remember the story?"

He either struggles to remember or fakes struggling to remember. "I think I might have heard something about it, but I had other stuff on my mind at the time."

"So you never saw the story or knew that Banner had done it?"

"I was in jail; how could I have seen the story? And I wouldn't know Banner if he walked in this room."

"He won't be walking in any more rooms. He was shot in the back of the head like Zimmer and Hackett . . . with the same gun."

"Holy shit. What the hell is going on?"

Since I have no idea what the hell is going on, I don't bother answering the question. Instead I ask, "Where were you the night of November twenty-first?"

"I have no idea."

"Do you have a calendar that you could consult?"

"Sure. It's in my office at the shop, but I didn't always keep it up-to-date. Mostly, but not always. I can have Chuck Holmes drop it off for you."

"That's okay; I'll stop by and pick it up. Just please let him know that I'll be by tomorrow." I don't mention that Chuck didn't seem inclined to leave when he dropped off the key at my office. This way our next encounter will be on his turf, so I'll be in charge of exit timing. I am really good at leaving meetings.

I head home for dinner with Laurie and Ricky, after which I walk Tara and Sebastian. Laurie has made my favorite, delivered pizza, and I down five pieces, crust included. Laurie only has two pieces and doesn't eat the crusts, which is why Laurie looks like Laurie and Andy looks like Andy.

School is closed for Christmas vacation, so when I get back we drop Ricky off at his friend Will Rubenstein's for a sleepover. This gives us a chance to go to Tony Birch's house and get a sense of the layout.

Tony's house is in the Radburn section of Fair Lawn, less than fifteen minutes from our house. It's a nice, well-maintained neighborhood, which would be more important if we were looking to buy a house. We're not; we're looking to see how hard it is to notice someone burying a gun.

The inside of the house has that "searched-in" look: the cops did not exactly take great care to put everything back exactly as they found it. But that's okay, we're not interested in what's on the inside. We want the view to the outside.

We start to look around and Laurie says, "Must be upstairs," so that's where we go.

Sure enough, Tony's bedroom is upstairs. The bed is unmade; he probably didn't realize then that the last time he slept in it might actually be the last time he sleeps in it. Or maybe he's like me: the last time I made a bed was because I was told that if I didn't, I couldn't play Little League baseball.

We go in and head right for the window to see what his view of his backyard would be.

We can see about half the yard from this bedroom, since it's on the side of the house. It's dark out there, and the only light that's illuminating it is coming from the bedroom that we're in. Laurie turns the switch off, and the yard is completely dark.

We lock up the house and walk out to the yard itself. It's starting to drizzle lightly; it's in the high thirties and too warm for snow. "If it was a clear night, the moonlight would have made it easier to see," Laurie says. "I'll check what the weather was for that night when we get home."

She has a flashlight, and when she turns it off, we are standing in almost total darkness. "Where was the gun buried?" she asks.

"The discovery said ten feet north of the garage and seven feet from the back fence."

She turns the flashlight back on and steps it off. "Right here."

We both look up at the house; we are not standing in a place where Tony could have seen this area from his bedroom, if he really was in his bedroom.

"He had no sight line, and we're far enough that if someone was quiet, he wouldn't have heard them, particularly if he was asleep," she says.

"I agree."

"Chalk up one victory for our side."

"A small one."

She smiles. "Hopefully the first of many."

Laurie turns, and as she does, the flashlight turns with her, briefly illuminating the area on the side of the garage, before it moves past it. Then she turns off the flashlight, but not before I thought I saw something.

"Turn it back on. Aim it high up on the garage." What I saw was not at the top, but rather at the bottom.

But I don't want her to shine the light directly on it, in case I'm wrong. Reflected light will tell us what we need to know.

She does what I ask, and there, sitting next to the base of garage, is what I was hoping I had seen.

Zoey.

Zoey looks frightened and hungry and wary.

We have got to get her to come to us; if we approach her, she might bolt, and then we'd be back where we started.

"Biscuits," Laurie says, and I instantly know what she means. We keep a box of biscuits in the car for when we go places with Tara and Sebastian. I slowly walk to the car to get them; no sudden movement and no slamming the car door. I also grab a leash; if we get lucky, we'll get to use it.

I walk back and hand the biscuits and leash to Laurie; we both silently understand that she is going to have to take the lead here. Dogs, like humans, would instinctively rather be with Laurie than with me. But she gives the leash back to me, obviously thinking that Zoey might find it threatening.

The yard is not fenced in, so Zoey has plenty of available exits if she chooses to run. She is either going to voluntarily come with us, or not at all.

Laurie starts to say, "Hi, Zoey. Hi, sweet girl," in a high-pitched voice. Laurie walks slowly toward her, continuing saying the words and showing her the biscuits. This is the most nervous I've been in a while.

It seems like it takes forever. Laurie is about two feet from her, which is the same as a mile if Zoey takes off. Laurie is holding out one of the biscuits, while continuing to talk and continuing to advance.

Laurie goes into a crouch, still holding the biscuit out. As Eddie Dowd might put it, the ball is on Zoey's racquet . . . it's all up to her. Laurie's body has stopped moving, but her arm gradually and slowly extends, until the biscuit is just inches from Zoey's mouth.

Slowly but surely, mouth moves toward biscuit until Zoey takes it. Laurie's right hand slowly offers another biscuit, while her left hand equally slowly moves to pet Zoey's head. My internal voice is screaming at her to grab the collar, but she doesn't. She must still sense that Zoey could escape and run.

But then she does take hold of the collar, still petting Zoey the whole time. There is a sudden loud sound, and I realize it is me exhaling.

In a soft voice that sounds a little weird, Laurie says, "Bring the leash, Andy."

I do so, walking carefully, and Laurie takes it with her right hand. Her left is still grasping the collar. She gently puts the leash over Zoey's neck and stands up. "We can go now," Laurie says, in that weird voice again. It finally hits me that she sounds like that because she is crying.

We put Zoey into the backseat of the car, and Laurie gets back there as well, so she can hold and comfort her. "We must be twenty-five miles from Willie's house," I say. "How the hell did she find this place?"

"She really loves Tony."

Without either of us saying anything, we both realize we need to head straight for Willie's house. I call ahead to tell Willie and Sondra what has happened and that we're coming; I don't want them to be upset for a single second longer than necessary.

Sondra answers and I quickly tell her what's going on. "Oh, Andy . . . please hurry." She starts sobbing and hangs up.

When we get to their house, Willie and Sondra are outside waiting for us. Willie opens the back door and Laurie hands him the leash; he holds it so tight I don't think Marcus could break his grip. Sondra spends some time hugging Zoey and crying, and then I say, "You should get her into the house."

Sondra nods. "I'll take her. Laurie, Andy . . . thank you so much." Sondra then takes her inside.

Willie turns to us and says, "You guys are the best," and follows her in.

"Let's go home and pet our dogs," Laurie says.

I haven't heard a better idea in a while.

Between Corey and Laurie, they must know every cop in New Jersey, if not America.

Corey had contacted a friend of his in the Jersey City Police Department who he says has information about Terry Banner that might be interesting to us. Corey's heading there with me now, probably because he's seen me interact with police and knows that on my own I'm more likely to get shot than I am to get information.

Corey has brought Simon along because Corey brings Simon anywhere he's allowed, and some places he isn't. Simon gets by because he has that police dog vibe, not surprising since he was a working police dog for almost seven years. Corey would tell you that he loves Simon as much as I love Tara, which is impossible, since no one loves anything or anyone as much as I love Tara.

On the way to Jersey City, Corey tells me that Lieutenant Chris Guerrero used to be his partner on the Paterson police force, but left about six years ago because he saw a better opportunity for advancement in Jersey City. The name is familiar to me, but I can't place it.

Unfortunately, Lieutenant Guerrero's memory is better

than mine. As soon as he sees me, he says, "Oh, shit." Then he turns to Corey and asks, 'This was the lawyer you told me about?"

"You two know each other?" Corey asks.

By now I've realized that I brutalized then Sergeant Guerrero on a cross-examination at least eight years ago. "We ran into each other once," I say.

Guerrero sneers. "Ran into each other. I wanted to run you over with a truck. Actually, that still seems like the best option."

"That's the Christmas spirit."

"Christmas is over," he says, almost snarling.

"That depends on who you ask."

Guerrero looks like he is about to tear my head off, but the tension is semi-broken when Simon goes over to him, wagging his tail and accepting petting. "Simon, old buddy, good to see you." Guerrero obviously remembers Simon more fondly than he does me.

"So you said you had information about Terry Banner's murder," Corey says. "I thought Andy should hear it at the same time."

Guerrero shakes his head. "Not about the murder; just about Banner."

I'm not surprised to hear this. Banner was murdered in Scranton and we're sitting in Jersey City, 120 miles away. "Whatever you have is good," I say.

He stares at me with disdain. "Thank you. I crave your approval."

"That's what I'm here for."

Corey shakes his head. "Boys, boys . . ." Then, "Tell us about Banner."

"Okay. When he was working at Channel Five in New York, he lived in Hoboken. He made more money off camera than on."

"Drugs?" I ask.

Guerrero nods. "Drugs. He worked both ends; he took them and he sold them. With an emphasis on *sold* them."

"Did you guys go after him?"

"No, he wasn't really on our radar until after he left. We only learned about it because a gang informant mentioned it. We forwarded the information to the Scranton police, but I don't know what they did with it."

"Hard to imagine that fresh Scranton air convinced him to change his lifestyle," I say.

"Can we get access to the informant?" Corey asks.

"Maybe in the next life. His body was found in a park not too far from here a long time ago. We never did locate his head. Luther was sending a message that 'gang informant' is a dangerous job description."

"Where was Luther's base of operations?" I ask.

"He has a few places of business, and before he consolidated his base, he moved around a lot. Now he's mostly in Passaic. I can get you the information we have on him."

"That would be great," Corey says.

"Let me ask you this," I say. "Is Luther the type to order a hit and then frame someone else for it?"

Guerrero thinks for a moment. "Seems unlikely, but it's always possible. Especially if Luther would be the guy they would otherwise look at first."

"You said he consolidated his base. What does that mean, exactly?" I ask.

"Over the years he built up his strength, and I'm talking about manpower, money, and weapons. He backed it up with a fairly unique ruthlessness; this guy will kill anyone in his way, and I'd bet he never loses any sleep over it.

"So he slowly moved in on smaller street gangs. In some cases they offered no resistance and started working for him. It became a well-paid, steady job for most of them. In other cases, gangs tried to defend their turf. That didn't work out too well; usually whoever was their leader wound up dead or permanently missing.

"It became easier and safer to come aboard. He let the gangs maintain their turf, at least in their minds, but he was calling the important shots. They paid him royalties; think of it as a franchise operation. Like McDonald's, only criminal and violent."

This fits in exactly with what Tony was saying about the Fulton Street Boyz, the gang he was in. Clearly they were in the group that did not contest Luther's entrance onto their turf, but rather became his employees. Tony's claim was that the attempted collection on Josh Winkler, which resulted in the child's death, made him realize this was a step too far.

"How has he interacted with organized crime?" Corey asks. I know that he's talking about the more traditional Mafia-style operations, mostly controlled in this area by Joseph Russo, Jr.

"It's evolving," Guerrero says. "At first the old-schoolers were dominant, and the gangs, even Luther, were confined to smaller-time street action. But as we started taking the traditional guys down, the gangs filled in the void. Now they pretty much maintain separate operations. There are occasional flare-ups, but neither side wants to push it too far."

"So what are the chances of taking Luther down?"

Guerrero frowns. "Right now? Very small. He does none of the dirty work himself, and those who do would rather go to prison than turn on him. They want to keep living."

Corey drops me off at my office, because that's where my car is.

Eddie Dowd is there working and going over documents, which impresses me.

I take the time to go over the limited progress I've made in recent days. One of the weaknesses of my management style is that I don't always keep everyone up-to-date.

I tell him about my meeting with Guerrero, and with Josh Winkler.

"Did you believe Winkler?" he asks.

"Yes, I think so. He was up-front about his connection to Luther, and why he was involved in that incident that night."

Sam comes in to see if there's any other assignments he needs to handle; he's hoping they will involve using his gun. I do have something for him, but it's tamer than he'd like.

"Actually, yes; I meant to mention this to you before. See what you can find out about Russell Estrada. He's one of Luther's right-hand men in the Blood Dragons. He was the contact between Luther and Tony's group. He gave the order to collect from Josh Winkler the night the little girl died."

Sam nods. "I'm on it, Chief."

Eddie and I talk about it for a few minutes more and then I leave him there. My first stop is at Tony's shop to pick up his calendar. His employee, Chuck Holmes, is sitting at the desk when I get there. No cars are in the work area, which is not a good sign for an auto repair shop.

"Hello, Mr. Carpenter, I've got Mr. Tony's calendar right here." He hands me an envelope.

"Thanks, Chuck. Business is quiet?"

He nods. "Been like this for a while."

"Hopefully it will pick up," I say, though there is absolutely no hope of that at all. People tend to stop patronizing and supporting people who they think are double or triple murderers.

"I think so too. Mr. Tony be back soon?"

"We're working on it." I turn to leave, then ask, "Chuck, are you getting paid for working here? I mean, since Tony left."

He shrugs. "It's no problem; Mr. Tony be back soon."

"I'll make sure you get paid, Chuck. By tomorrow."

I leave and call Eddie to ask him to find out from Tony how much Chuck makes, and the last time he was paid. I'm going to have to pay him myself; clearly the business is not generating money. Nor is the Birch case proving to be particularly lucrative for his attorney.

But I feel bad for Chuck. Tony's presence is obviously essential for the survival of the business. If he doesn't get cleared, it will go under, and Chuck will be out of a job, with no money coming in. Christmas is a bad time for that to happen. Any time is a bad time for that to happen.

In my ongoing effort to meet every single cop who has ever worked in New Jersey, I'm heading to Pete Stanton's office. He's set up a meeting with George Koontz, a former homicide cop. His last three years on the force he served under Pete, and I know Pete has kept up with him since he retired.

I get there before Koontz and head back to Pete's office. It's nice of him to have set up this meeting; favors from homicide cops to defense attorneys are not an everyday occurrence. Maybe I'm finally getting returns on the four million burgers and beers I've been buying for him.

"George says he doesn't know you, never ran into you on a case."

"That's good," I say.

"He also says he's heard about you."

"That's bad."

Koontz arrives and seems pleasant enough. He greets Pete with a big hug; Pete must have been a good boss. I get a firm handshake and a smile, which is better than expected.

"I've missed this place," Koontz says.

"You were just here two weeks ago for Barone's retirement party," Pete says.

"I missed it then too."

They go through some more insufferable cop small talk, and Pete finally says, "Andy's got some questions for you. I should warn you that even for a defense attorney, he's irritating and obnoxious."

I make a waving motion with my hand. "Aw, come on, enough about me."

"Let her rip," Koontz says, undaunted by Pete's warning.

"I want to talk about Tony Birch. You remember him?"

"Of course. I remember every case I ever handled. That was an easy one. From what I see on the news, he sure as hell did not learn his lesson."

"He got in a street fight and killed a guy back then. He said it was self-defense."

"And two witnesses said otherwise," Koontz says. "Two witnesses who up to that point were friends of his. He got lucky with involuntary manslaughter. Should have been murder."

Pete jumps in unhelpfully with "Andy is representing him. He says he's innocent; isn't that a shocker?"

Koontz laughs a fake laugh. "Yeah, major surprise."

"I'm just here to talk about the case you handled, but I'm not relitigating it. You say he was guilty, that's fine with me. He served his time."

"So what then?"

"I want to talk about the victim in that case. Melvin Garza."

"G-Bop."

"G-Bop?"

"That's what everybody called him. I guess he wasn't too big on the sound of *Melvin*."

"The media reports said that he was a carpenter."

"Yeah. And I'm the king of Denmark."

"So would Your Excellency know what his actual job was?" I ask.

"He was a gangbanger, like your client."

"What gang?"

"You mean their name? Who the hell knows or cares?"

"That wasn't part of the investigation?" I ask.

"Maybe at one point we knew, but now I don't remember. And there was no point at which it was relevant. What happened in the street that night was the only fact we needed."

"The fact that the victim was in a street gang wasn't a significant fact to consider?"

Koontz turns to Pete. "You were right about this guy; he's a pain in the ass."

"It didn't take great insight," Pete says.

Koontz once again addresses me. "Look, the guy was in a gang, so what? Who do you think you're going to run into in that part of town at two o'clock in the morning, Mother Teresa? The law says you can't kill anyone, including gang members. In fact, that's why your client is currently in jail."

I ignore the question; this guy is getting on my nerves, so I want to bring this to a conclusion. "Could it have been the Blood Dragons?"

Koontz thinks about it for a good fifteen seconds. "I just don't remember. But whether it was or not isn't the point, because they controlled most of the gangs in that area. So he was either a member of the Dragons or he probably worked for them."

"Do you know what started the fight?"

"No. Your guy wasn't talking, and the victim was too dead to provide much information. The two witnesses just heard arguing."

I've got all that I can get from Koontz, and it has actually been of some help. So I thank him and Pete and stand to leave.

"You coming to Charlie's tonight?" Pete asks.

"No . . . way too busy."

"You're not going to Charlie's on New Year's Eve? What the hell has happened to you?"

"It's called adulthood, Pete." I had actually forgotten that it was New Year's Eve; Laurie and I always just stay home and watch the celebrations on TV with Ricky. "Besides, I know it's a romantic evening for you and Vince, so I don't want to be the third wheel and spoil it."

Pete ignores the insult. "We'll miss you, but we'll have your tab to remember you by." Then, to Koontz, "You up for some free food and beer tonight? There's an open seat at Charlie's."

"Sounds good. Can I bring a buddy?"

"Of course," Pete says. "Tell him to come hungry and thirsty."

Luther and the Blood Dragons seem to be under every rock we turn over.

Tony, Zimmer, and Hackett were all employed by Luther, as was TJ Richardson, who shot the child by accident. TJ wound up dead in prison, which was decidedly not an accident.

Terry Banner was also connected to Luther through drugs. Luther was his contact for the drugs, both for his personal use and, more important, for resale. If Banner was making a lot of money from that action, as Lieutenant Guerrero said he was, then Luther must have come out pretty well also.

Maybe Banner decided that making payment was overrated, which could have caused Luther to kill him. Or maybe Banner was stupid enough to try to cut Luther out entirely. The list of things that could have gotten Banner killed is rather long; drug dealing is a dangerous business.

Lastly, the guy that Tony killed in that street fight years ago was either in the Blood Dragons or worked for them. Neither would ingratiate Tony with Luther; I'm actually surprised that Tony survived his time in prison.

Having said all that, I'm still not seeing Luther framing someone as his method of punishment. The theory that we are building weighs heavily against that being the case. If we believe that Luther killed Zimmer, Hackett, and Banner, then why would we think he'd have a different fate planned for Tony?

That's not to say it couldn't be the case. Maybe Luther views life in prison as a more horrifying punishment than a bullet in the head. Maybe he has both penalties planned for Tony, starting with a stretch in prison and then ending with a prison murder.

It's also possible that it's someone else in the hierarchy of the Blood Dragons that is behind this. I don't know enough about the inner workings of that gang—in fact I know nothing about the inner workings of that gang—to make an educated guess about whether that is likely or even possible.

Maybe one of Luther's people is operating on his own, or maybe at Luther's direction. I know what I'll do. I'll get Luther on the stand and ask, "Luther, did you order the Code Red?" And he'll scream, "You're goddamn right I did!"

The way things are shaping up, Luther and the Blood Dragons are going to be at the center of whatever case we are able to mount. One of the best ways to get a jury to have reasonable doubt as to a defendant's guilt is to have someone else to point to.

My belief is that a key barrier to getting a jury to acquit is that they are then left with the feeling that the murder is going to go unpunished. They want someone to blame, so that they can tell themselves that they are teeing it up for another jury to convict the real killer.

No one is going to consider Luther incapable of murder. Just the name of the gang he heads, the Blood Dragons, conjures up violence. If we were trying to deflect guilt to Sylvia and the Canasta Ladies, it would be a higher mountain to climb. Luther and the Blood Dragons comes in with the presumption of violence.

But we're going to have to learn more about them, and that in itself can be a dangerous operation. Enter Marcus Clark, my trusted Vice President in Charge of Danger Management. Laurie has asked him to come over around dinnertime for a strategy session.

I was never in the army, but I imagine that preparing to serve Marcus dinner is something like getting ready to feed an infantry division after a day of intense training. The last time we had him over he ate three entrées, a plate, two forks, and part of a sofa bed.

Marcus arrives and spends some time greeting Ricky, who is clearly delighted to see him. Laurie and Ricky are the only people I know of on the planet who are not afraid of Marcus. The feeling is obviously mutual; he even smiles when he's in their presence. I don't know how to explain it other than that there's a Jekyll and Marcus thing going on.

Laurie cooks enough pasta to feed Argentina, and I bring three pizzas in as a backup. We wind up having enough, but it's touch and go for a while. After dinner we go in the den, and Laurie brings Marcus up to date on our situation. Ricky goes off to his room to pretend to work on a book report he'll have to hand in when school vacation ends.

She asks Marcus if he is familiar with Luther, and he nods and grunts something indecipherable. Laurie has always been able to understand Marcus's strange speech habits, so they have a conversation about what we want him to do.

Basically, Marcus's assignment is to learn as much as he can about Luther's day-to-day operation, including where he works out of and where he lives. If we ever plan to approach him, and I sincerely hope we don't, then Marcus will figure out the best way to do it.

Ricky comes in and asks if "Uncle Marcus" can put him to bed tonight. Marcus is more than happy to do so, and he spends ten minutes in Ricky's room. I can hear the sound of Ricky laughing all the way down the hall.

Marcus is a good guy and he scares the shit out of me.

It's hard for me to comprehend the pain of losing a child.

And of all the awful ways it could happen, maybe none are worse than the way it happened to the Sanford family. One minute they were leaving a restaurant in the early evening, and the next minute their eight-year-old daughter, Julie, was dead on the street, a bullet having passed directly through her heart.

I have been trying to find people that might have a grudge against Tony Birch, and the Sanfords have to be on the list. He didn't fire the shot, that was done by TJ Richardson. But it came out in the trial that Zimmer, Hackett, and Tony were Richardson's buddies in the gang. Richardson, Zimmer, and Hackett are now dead, and only Tony is left.

Laurie tried to get Julie's mother to talk to us, but she refused. I can't say I blame her, but I would like to at least check the box that rules out anyone connected to the Sanfords as someone who has been behind our case.

If Laurie can't get a person's cooperation, then no one can. But she is resourceful, so she managed to get Julie's older sister, Donna, to agree to speak with us. Donna works as a paralegal for a law firm in Paramus, so we're meeting her after work at a coffee shop near there.

She's already there when we arrive, and she waves us over to her table. "I recognized you from television," she says.

I've made some TV appearances on a few high-profile cases, which I assume is what she's talking about. Unless she's confusing me with one of those guys on *The Bachelor.* Probably not.

We go through the hellos and order coffee. "Thanks for talking with us," Laurie says. "I know it can't be easy."

"None of it was anything close to easy, and I'm not sure I should be here at all. But I don't have a reason to have anything against your client; at least nothing that I know of. He wasn't the one that fired the shot that killed Julie. He wasn't there, right?"

Laurie nods. "I understand, Donna. But you're right; he was not involved in any way with what happened to your sister."

"Did he kill those two people?"

"We don't believe he did," I say.

"So what do you want from me?"

"We just have a few questions; maybe you can at least point us in the right direction."

She nods a bit warily. "What are they?"

"You weren't there the night Julie died, correct?" Laurie is going to do most of the questioning. It requires some sensitivity, and I don't generally carry any around with me.

Donna nods. "That's right. I had a date. I heard about what happened on the radio, but they didn't give a name.

But I knew that they had gone to that theater that night, and I had a terrible premonition, so I went home right away."

"What a horrible experience."

"Beyond anything I could have imagined," Donna says. "She was such a wonderful little girl, and little sister. . . ."

I can see her eyes starting to tear up. This is a pain that will never go away.

Donna continues, "Julie died and our family was destroyed."

"What happened?" Laurie asks.

"My parents broke up; they just couldn't keep it together after that. I don't think it was that they blamed each other; it was more that they blamed themselves. Which was crazy; what is wrong with taking your daughter to a movie? My father died in a car crash two years later; I've always thought it was a form of passive suicide . . . or maybe not so passive.

"My mother has never been the same . . . not even close. She cut herself off from all her friends, from the rest of our family, even from me. She sits home all day, bitter and shattered. My brother, he's three years older than me, couldn't deal with it and just left. He never looked back. I think he was the smartest of us for doing it."

"What is your brother's name?" Laurie asks.

"Richie. Richie Sanford."

"And you haven't heard from him in all that time?" I ask.

Donna shakes her head. "No, and I'm sure my mother hasn't either. Richie had pulled away from the family even before Julie died. He was . . . I guess you'd say troubled . . . trying to find himself and not knowing where to look. Julie . . . well, that was the last straw for him; he had to get away."

Time for me to jump in. "Donna, we're terribly sorry for what you and your family went through; it is unimaginably awful. And we're also very sorry to dredge it up again and make you talk about it."

"It's okay. In a way it helps."

"Thank you for that. I'm going to be honest with you. We are trying to identify people that could have motive for revenge against our client, as well as the two men that were murdered."

She seems confused. "None of those people killed Julie."

"I know," I say. "But there might be some people that wouldn't have your clear-eyed perspective."

"If you're asking if anyone I know could have killed those people, there's no way. We are not strong enough."

"What about friends, members of your extended family . . . ?" I'm grasping at straws and regretting that we came.

Donna shakes her head with some determination. "No. There's simply no way."

I drop Laurie off and head down to the office.

I want to finish reading through the discovery documents on Hackett's death, and I also need time to think. I don't have discovery for Terry Banner's murder since it's not part of our trial.

Unfortunately, Tony's calendar is blank for the night Banner took a bullet in the head. While he can't be charged for the murder in New Jersey, if there was evidence clearing him of it, that could have a major impact on our case. Certainly it would have created reasonable doubt about Tony's guilt in a jury's mind: if someone else had used that gun in Pennsylvania, chances were good that the same person used it in New Jersey.

But while Banner's murder isn't somehow a get-out-of-jail-free card for Tony, it is interesting in that it shows the depth and care that has gone into the frame-up. Whoever killed Banner most likely knew that Tony would not have an alibi for that night, since not to have known would have risked their entire operation.

That means that Tony was under surveillance, which in turn likely means that the framers have considerable resources. They would have had to be watching Tony in New Jersey while killing Banner in Pennsylvania. It doesn't have to have been that way, but it makes the most sense.

Luther has those resources ten times over. He has ample people at his disposal to have easily accomplished the surveillance and the killing simultaneously. That's not to say he's the only one that could have done it, but it's still another factor pointing in his direction. He might also not have realized that the Banner homicide could not be included or even mentioned in our trial; that's a legality that most people wouldn't realize.

Hovering over all of this is another person who could by definition have easily done it . . . Tony Birch.

I'm only in my office for thirty seconds when Sam comes in. He always seems to know when I'm here; maybe he has a bug planted somewhere. Sam is certainly capable of planting it, and I'm certainly capable of not detecting it.

"You have a bug planted in here, Sam?"

"Actually a webcam; I'm trying to get a video of Edna working. But I've been trying for three years and I haven't pulled it off yet."

I nod. "A working Edna. It's like the Loch Ness Monster or the yeti."

He laughs. "Exactly." Then, "You think the office is bugged? I could check it out."

"No, I was just kidding. You always seem to know when I arrive."

"The way you clomp up the steps it sounds like the Russian army. You're not a glider, Andy."

"I know; Laurie refuses to dance with me. As long as you're here, I've got something for you."

"Roger that." As soon as we start talking about a case, Sam morphs into Dick Tracy.

"An eight-year-old girl named Julie Sanford was killed by a stray bullet during a gun battle on the street. A guy named TJ Richardson was the killer, and he was found guilty and sent to prison.

"Julie Sanford had a brother named Richie; he was considerably older than her. The death apparently tore the family apart, and Richie is said to have left home and never looked back. I want to know if that's true, or if in fact he did look back."

"So you don't know where he is?"

"I don't. Let me know what you can find out about him, and where he might be living."

"I'm all over it. Anything else?"

"Yes, I've been meaning to check on this for a while. Tony went to the Crown Bar the night that Zimmer was killed. He said that Zimmer had called him earlier in the day and asked him to meet him there. You should check Tony's phone records and see if you can confirm that." Sam can get into any phone records he wants; if I had that ability, I'd never pay another phone bill.

"Okay. I'll check Zimmer's phone as well, so I can go at it from both ends."

"You know Zimmer's phone number?"

"Andy . . ."

"Sorry. I must not question the master."

"That's better. I'll get right on this," Sam says, then leaves.

It's a shot in the dark to think that Julie's brother might have come back to get revenge against someone like Tony, who didn't actually shoot his sister. But since Tony is being accused of literally shooting in the dark, it somehow seems appropriate.

Laurie calls and tells me that Marcus is ready to tell us what he has learned about Luther and a possible way to get at him. Marcus is coming over after dinner tonight to update us. She is going to have Corey come by as well; if we're going to mount any kind of operation against Luther, we might want all hands on deck.

Of course, if it comes to that, then I won't be on the actual deck; I'll be paddling away in a lifeboat with the women and children.

Marcus has learned quite a bit about Luther in a short time.

At least that seems to be the case as he gives his report, but I can't be sure because I don't understand more than one of every five words he is saying. I can tell that Corey doesn't either because he and I make eye contact, conveying our mutual confusion.

Fortunately, Laurie is here to receive and translate the information, and it is impressive. Luther is believed to have more than 150 people in his direct or indirect employ. Of those, less than 45 are in the actual Blood Dragons gang; the rest are in the various offshoots that have come under the wing of the, shall we say, parent company.

Luther's criminal activities are the old standbys: drugs, gambling, and prostitution. He is also thought to be running a protection racket, demanding retail-business owners pay a fee to avoid the difficulties that nonpayment can bring about.

Luther himself no longer does any of the dirty work; he functions as the chief executive officer. He does not maintain a corporate headquarters, though. Instead, he works out of three offices, all located in the back rooms of bars that he is believed to own. His name is not on the paperwork, but he is in control of each of the three locations.

His offices are located in Passaic, Newark, and Elizabeth, though he spends more time in the Passaic branch than the others. Possibly that is to keep potential enemies off-balance, though he does not seem to be facing any serious threats.

Interestingly, all this success has led Luther to enjoy some of the finer things. According to Marcus he lives on an estate in Alpine, among doctors and lawyers and investment bankers. I don't know if he associates with his neighbors, or if they know who their neighbor is.

When it comes to restaurants, Luther frequents a select few. Marcus assumes that is because he feels safe in these particular spots and has some control over the environment. Marcus doesn't know if Luther owns a piece of each of those restaurants, but it wouldn't be surprising.

Bottom line is that we are not dealing with Riff or Bernardo and the Sharks or the Jets. This is the natural evolution of street gangs owning the streets. Eventually they will fold over and feed on themselves, and law enforcement will hasten that process. They will fade, as organized crime has faded, as individual self-interest comes into play.

But that will happen later, or it might not happen at all. Either way, we have no time to sit around and wait for it.

We kick around ideas about what we can do with the information that Marcus has brought us. We are running out of time; the trial is bearing down on us and we currently have no bullets in our defense gun.

Luther is going to have to be a part of that defense, whether or not he and his gang have any real-life culpability. We are going to have to point to him because we don't have any other options.

Marcus is confident that we can get to him; Marcus is always confident we can get to anybody. And the cool thing about Marcus is that he is always right.

But we need to have a reason to do so; just going barreling in does not by itself accomplish anything. It has to result in our getting information that we can put before a jury and advance our cause. I just don't see where we have that dilemma solved yet.

Marcus leaves, and Corey and I take Simon, Tara, and Sebastian for a walk. Laurie stays home with Ricky, telling us that while we're gone, she is going to work on the tree. For Laurie, the Christmas tree is a work in progress; she is constantly tinkering with the lights and ornaments. This goes on for the entire four-month Christmas holiday.

Corey and I don't talk much, mainly because I like to spend these walks thinking. I don't think well when my mouth is moving.

Finally I say, "Luther has too many layers surrounding him; we're going to have to rattle his cage."

"His cage won't rattle easily."

"I know that. And I can't even clearly see a way that it can play out in our favor."

"But you want to do it anyway," Corey says, more a statement than a question.

"Yes."

"Why?"

"Because the alternative is to do nothing."

We're quiet for a few minutes, then Corey asks, "The prosecution has a really strong case. Did you ever consider the possibility that they are right? That Birch murdered those people?"

"Of course I have."

"And where do you come out?"

"Willie and Zoey both believe in him, and they know him a hell of a lot better than I do. So I'm going with them, and if they're wrong, then I'm wrong. I'll just have to be okay with that."

Patty Garza was our second choice for this interview. Laurie had attempted to set up an interview with Melvin Garza's brother, Johnny. Melvin was the gang member whom Tony killed in a street fight, resulting in his involuntary manslaughter conviction. Melvin, as I was informed by George Koontz, the cop who worked the case, was known as G-Bop.

I don't know what they call Johnny Garza, and I'm not likely to find out. When Laurie called, she reached Johnny's wife, Patty. Patty told Laurie that trying to get Johnny to talk to Tony Birch's lawyer would be inviting disaster. When Laurie pressed the matter, Patty agreed to talk to me, but not at their house.

So I'm waiting for Patty at the Allwood Diner in Clifton, just a few blocks from where she lives. I'm just going to have coffee, which is a good thing, because if I was having dinner, it would take me an hour and a half to choose from the quarter of a million options on the menu.

It's a large place, so I tell the woman at the desk who I'm waiting for. She says that she knows Patty and will send her to my table when she arrives. The woman does exactly that, about ten minutes later.

Patty Garza is petite, maybe thirty years old, with a pretty but tired face. My guess is she has worked all day, which she confirms by telling me with an apologetic smile that she "got stuck in the office."

"No problem," I say. "I won't take too much of your time. You want something to eat?"

"No, I'm going to make dinner tonight. I'll just have some coffee."

I signal to the waitress and ask her to bring the coffee, which she does.

"I'm sorry," Patty says. "I know you wanted to talk to Johnny, but believe me that would not have been a good idea."

"Because I am representing Tony Birch?"

She nods. "Yes. Johnny hates him for what he did. I hope you can understand that."

Since Tony went to jail for killing Johnny's brother, I can certainly understand that, and I tell her so. "I didn't know Tony then," I say, "but I know he paid for his crime."

She nods. "Three years. Melvin is paying for it a lot longer than that."

"Yes, he is. And I'm sorry." I'd better move this along, before she convinces me to prosecute Tony. "I believe Tony is being wrongly accused this time, and someone is setting that up deliberately. I am trying to find out who that might be."

"And you think that could be Johnny?"

"I don't know Johnny. It could be anyone, and I was

hoping you could point me in a direction, if you have any ideas. I'm sure Melvin must have had friends who were very upset and still are."

She frowns. "Melvin did not live what you would call a clean life. I actually didn't know him for very long; he died . . . he was killed . . . just a year after I met Johnny. But I know he hung around with people who could be described as . . . well . . . dangerous. Johnny does not live in that world. Johnny works hard and is a good husband."

"Is there anyone specific you can think of that might be prone to this kind of revenge?"

"I'm afraid I don't. . . . I can't help you with that."

"If you could think about—"

"She said that she can't help you with that." It's a voice from behind me to the left. I turn and see an angry face, sitting on top of a tall, well-built body. I know that this is Johnny Garza as surely as I know I am Andy Carpenter. With him over my left shoulder, I wish Marcus was over my right shoulder, but he isn't.

"Patty, I told you not to talk to this guy."

"And I told you I was going to." This is a young lady with some spunk.

He turns back to me, where he is likely to get less resistance. "Beat it."

"We are just having a conversation," I say.

"Not anymore. I'm warning you."

"You should probably go, Mr. Carpenter," Patty says.

Those are my sentiments exactly; I've pretty much gotten all I'm going to get from this interview anyway. "Okay. Thanks for your time."

I summon as much dignity as I can and head for the exit. I stop at the front desk and give the woman a fifty-dollar bill. "Please tell Johnny and Patty that dinner is on me."

She smiles. "I will."

am meeting Sam at the office at 10:00 A.M.

He's ready to give his report on the latest assignments I've given him. Sam works his computer magic with amazing speed; no cyber-grass grows under his feet.

Once again I stop and get doughnuts, three chocolate filled and three vanilla filled. Sam has already made coffee when I get there, and Edna is nowhere to be found. Edna's not being there is somehow comforting; it's a sign of consistency in a world that otherwise seems to have tilted off its axis.

"Let's start with the easy one, the question of whether Zimmer called Tony that day and told him to come down to the bar. The answer is that I don't see evidence of it, but it's possible."

"Explain, please."

"I will. Tony received only four calls that day, all on his cell phone. It was a Saturday, so his office was closed. Putting aside the question of how Zimmer would have known his cell phone number, none of the calls came from Zimmer's phone.

"However, one came from a number I can't trace back;

I'm assuming it's a burner phone, but I haven't confirmed that yet."

"It's possible," I say. "Zimmer might easily have been involved in criminal activities, so a burner phone might be useful. But I'm not sure why he would want to conceal a call to Tony."

"Zimmer made a lot of calls on his regular phone, that day and every other day. So if he used a burner, it was definitely a call he did not want traced back to him."

"Okay. What about Richie Sanford?"

"Interesting case. As best I can tell based on credit card records, when he left this area he went to Cincinnati. He stayed in a hotel for what looks like two weeks, and then he disappeared."

"Disappeared how?"

"Dropped off the grid. And it's almost impossible to drop off the grid, even if you die. He didn't die; there would be a record of that. More likely he changed his name."

I think about this for a few moments. On one level it's suspicious: people who change their names are often doing so to hide. But it can also be a way to break away from a previous life. It makes a clean break from whatever one is running away from. Maybe Richie Sanford wanted a clean slate, and maybe he didn't want to be found if his family tried to get him back. Donna Sanford had said he was troubled; maybe this was his attempt to put those troubles behind him.

"So no way to find him?"

Sam shakes his head. "I don't see how, without knowing his current identity. If he were to be arrested, his prints might give him away if they were on file, but short of that it will be very hard to find him. But I'll keep trying."

"Thanks, Sam. He was probably just doing what he needed to in order to stay sane."

Just then the phone rings, so I pick it up with my characteristically clever "Hello?"

"Mr. Carpenter?" It's a voice I don't recognize.

"That's me."

"This is Chuck Holmes. I work for Mr. Tony. I came to your office. . . ."

"Of course, Chuck. I know who you are."

"Mr. Carpenter, something happened. I . . ."

It clearly takes Chuck a long time to get to where he's conversationally going. "What happened, Chuck?"

"Somebody burned the shop."

"You mean where you work?"

"Yes."

"Are you there now?"

"Yes."

"Do you know who did it?"

"I think so. Maybe. But I don't know his name."

"Do you know how to find him?" I ask.

"No."

This is not going well. "What can you tell me about him?"

"I don't know . . . nothing, I guess." There is a pause. "But I have his picture."

"That'll work. Stay there; I'll be right down."

I call Laurie and ask her to meet me at Tony's office.

She says that she'll get there as soon as she can, but first she'll have to drop Ricky off at Will Rubenstein's house. We try to make an effort to take Ricky to as few crime scenes as possible.

When I arrive, the fire department is still doing their work, though the fire seems to have successfully been put out. They are basically making sure that no embers flare up and reignite the blaze. Although it doesn't look like there is much to save on the interior, I'm sure they are worried about the adjacent structures, which so far seem to have emerged unscathed.

I see Chuck Holmes standing across the street behind barricades that the fire department has constructed to keep people away and safe. He looks bewildered and a little scared, but brightens when he sees me.

"Let's go over there, Chuck." I point to an area on the corner, where no people are milling about.

He nods and follows me over there. "I didn't know who to call."

"You did the right thing. Tell me what happened."

"You mean with the fire? I don't know; I wasn't here when it started. We were closed today . . . we have no customers. I came down to get a jacket that was in the closet, but the fire department was already here. It was a big fire." Then, "I couldn't get my jacket."

"I understand. You said you think you know who did it?"

He frowns. "I think so, but maybe not. I just don't know. Mr. Tony is going to be very upset."

He looks like he is about to cry. "It's okay, Chuck. I'll talk to him."

"You'll tell him it wasn't my fault?"

"I will; nobody will blame you. He'll be glad that you're okay. Tell me about the man that you think did it. You have his picture?"

His mind seems to have wandered off, so I repeat what I said. Finally he nods and takes a folded photograph out of his pocket. It's a picture of a man, maybe thirty, standing at a counter. Because of the angle from above, my guess is it was taken by a surveillance camera.

"Was this taken in there?" I point toward the destroyed shop.

"Yes."

"When?"

"Yesterday. In the afternoon."

"Were you there?"

"No, I went out for lunch and I locked the door. When I came back, he was inside the shop; I don't know how he got in."

"What was he doing?"

"He was looking at Mr. Tony's desk."

"What did you do?"

"I told him that he wasn't allowed in there."

"What did he do?"

"He just looked at me; I thought he was going to hurt me. But then he walked out. He didn't say anything."

"You had cameras inside that took pictures?"

Chuck nods. "Mr. Tony did. I took the picture out of the camera; I didn't know what to do with it."

I see Laurie standing and talking to one of the cops helping out the firemen by guarding the scene. She nods to me to let me know she knows where I am.

I hold up the picture. "Have you ever seen this man before?"

Chuck shakes his head. "No. I don't think so."

"Chuck, I want you to do something for me. I want you to come to my office tomorrow at one o'clock in the afternoon, okay?"

"Am I in trouble?"

"No, you're not in trouble. Just come see me. I'll want to talk to you some more, and I'll also have your pay."

"Pay for what?"

"For working for Tony. None of this is your fault, Chuck. Now, will you come see me?"

He nods, though he doesn't seem comfortable with the idea. "I will."

"Okay. You did good, Chuck." I hold up the photograph. "I'm going to keep this until tomorrow."

He nods again and I start walking toward Laurie. She has just finished talking to the cop, and she walks toward me as well.

"Did you find out anything?" I ask.

"He overheard the fire department investigator. He said it's an obvious arson; gasoline was spread everywhere. No effort was made to hide it."

We agree that we'll talk further at home, so we leave. Laurie stops at Will Rubenstein's and winds up bringing both boys back to our house for what will become a sleepover. I spend the rest of the afternoon going through the case documents.

Once we've had dinner and the kids are settled in, I take Tara and Sebastian for their evening walk. When I get back, Laurie and I head into the den for some wine and romantic arson conversation.

I show Laurie the photograph that Chuck gave me; she does not recognize the person either.

"I'm going to show it to Tony," I say. "Hopefully he'll know who it is."

"What about the police?"

"Tomorrow. I'm going to have Chuck take it to them and tell them the story. It may or may not be related to our case, but if it is, I want it in the official record."

"Good. What does your gut say?"

"Unfortunately, I think the last time my gut was right was during the Clinton administration, but I think there was something that this guy wanted. Or more accurately, something that he didn't want anyone else to have. So when he got caught searching the desk, he decided to stop looking and just destroy everything."

"And do you think it's related to our case?"

"My gut doesn't think that far ahead."

His name is Russell Estrada; I told you about him. He works for Luther," Tony says. "What was he doing in my shop?"

Tony's identification of the photograph was instantaneous, as was his agitation level.

"I've got some bad news," I say. "There was a fire at your shop yesterday. The interior was pretty much destroyed."

His shock is evident. "What?" Then, "Was it arson? Did Estrada do it?"

"It was definitely arson, and I think it's quite possible that he was involved."

"Is Chuck okay?"

"Yes; he wasn't there when it happened. But he caught Estrada rifling through your desk the day before; that's when this picture was shot. It's reasonable but not yet provable to believe that he came back and started the fire."

"Why would he do that? I haven't seen him in years."

"That's a question that I want you to think about. If he was searching the place and then torched it, it would seem obvious that he thought you had something in your possession that was dangerous to him, or to his boss."

Tony thinks for a moment and then shakes his head. "I can't think of anything that I would have, or why he'd think I would."

"Tell me what you know about him."

"Not much. Like I said, he worked for Luther. I was told that Luther had three or four guys just under him who saw to it that things were carried out. Estrada was one of those guys."

"Was he your only contact?"

"Pretty much. For the entire time I was there."

"The incident with Josh Winkler that led to the Sanford girl being shot, you're sure that Estrada ordered that?"

"Yes. I don't ever remember getting assignments from anyone else."

"He was either looking for something that he thought you had—"

"I don't have anything like that, nothing left over from that time in my life."

"—or he was torching the place to get revenge or to hurt you. Any idea why he would want to do that?"

"No. I haven't seen or talked to the guy in years."

I can't get anything else out of Tony; he seems genuinely puzzled by why Estrada or anyone else would burn down his business. As I'm getting ready to leave, he says, "Chuck must be really scared. He doesn't do well with excitement."

"He seems okay. I'm going to be talking with him in a little while, so I'll make sure he's calm. How much does he make?"

"Until this all started, seven hundred a week. He's

actually a pretty good mechanic. I don't know what he'll do now."

"Don't worry about him; we'll make sure he's taken care of."

"You're going to pay him yourself?"

"Yes."

"You're unbelievable, Andy."

"Aw, shucks. Think some more about Estrada, and let me know if you come up with anything at all, whether you think it's important or not."

"Will do."

"By the way, did you have insurance on your place?"

"Yes. Not sure how I put in a claim from here."

"I'll ask Eddie Dowd to work on it."

I head back to the office. On the way I call Laurie and tell her that we have identified Estrada. "You should alert Marcus," I say. "We might want to talk to him before the police do."

"You think he'd tell us anything?"

"Us? No. But Marcus? Very possibly. As soon as Marcus walks into the room, I start to confess, and I haven't done anything wrong."

"What do you want him to say?"

"Turning on Luther would be nice."

"You really think that's possible? After everything we've heard about Luther?"

"We're talking about Marcus."

"Okay," she says, giving in. "I'll call him."

Eddie Dowd is already waiting for me at the office when I get there. I had asked him to be there when I met with Chuck. Chuck arrives precisely at 1:00 P.M.; I have a feeling that if I had set the meeting for 1:14, he would have arrived precisely at 1:14. This is a guy who takes direction and does not buck authority.

I introduce them and I tell Chuck that I just talked to Tony.

"Is he mad?"

"Not at all. He understands it wasn't your fault, and he is grateful to you for taking this photograph."

I can see the relief on Chuck's face. I take out the photograph and hand it to him. "I want you to give this to the police."

"Am I going to get into trouble?"

"Not at all; you're doing a good thing. Eddie is going to go with you; just listen to him and do what he says. When you talk to the police, just tell them what you told me yesterday, about how this man broke in and was going through Tony's desk."

"Okay."

I turn to Eddie. "Did you find out who is handling the police side of the arson investigation?"

He nods. "Sergeant Galeano."

"Good. Chuck should turn the information over to him. You're his lawyer, so you insist on being present. Don't say anything about Tony's case; they may have made the connection already, but we don't want to help them out. We may want to introduce all this in court later, and we want to have done the right thing by turning it over."

I don't mention this, but if I was the one to accompany Chuck when he turns over the photo, it would set off alarm bells. I want this done is as low-key a manner as possible.

Before they leave, I give Chuck a check for the past three weeks and the next two. "This is your salary from Mr. Tony."

He seems stunned. "But I haven't been working."

"Not your fault, Chuck. Not your fault."

We're going to have to pick up the pace.

The trial is bearing down on us. I don't know how long it will take Godfrey to put on his case; probably not long. But when he's finished, we'll have to be ready to present our defense. The main negative, as I see it, is that we don't currently have a defense.

But it's quite obvious that if we are going to develop one, it is going to center around Luther. That's not to say that Luther committed these particular murders, but he represents a credible person for us to point to.

But we can't just point; we also have to come up with rational arguments to support our position. And at this moment, those rational arguments are in short supply.

In fact, the entire Luther thing cuts both ways. Yes, he would be easy to portray as someone capable of the violent acts that Tony stands accused of. But the only way to connect Tony to him in the first place is to admit that Tony was in a gang, and that he and his cohorts did Luther's bidding.

So we tell the jury that Luther is bad and evil and

vicious and Tony was his loyal employee. That is not a winning argument.

The new piece to the puzzle is Russell Estrada's entry onto the scene and what seems to be his burning down of Tony's place of business. That he was nosing around Tony's desk when he was surprised by Chuck would seem to rule out revenge as a motive.

Estrada wanted something—or at least wanted to make sure that nobody else had it. Setting fire to it must have seemed like a sure way to guarantee that. The question is what he might have been after; Tony claims not to know. That doesn't mean that he's telling the truth; whatever it is could be just as dangerous to Tony as it seems to be to Russell.

I've been operating in investigative mode so far, and that will at least partially continue, but now it's time to put on my lawyer uniform. I need to be fully and completely informed about the facts of the case so that I can be prepared in the moment for any eventuality during the trial.

We're about to be in court, where total, instant recall is essential. Lawyers who after the fact say to themselves "That's what I should have said" do not win cases.

So after dinner I will head into the den to read over all the documents. I've read them twice already and will do so many times more before the case is over. Each time I try to look at them with a fresh eye, which is not an easy trick to pull off.

I like working in the den this time of year. If I close the doors, I don't have to hear Nat King Cole "offering a simple phrase, for kids from one to ninety-two." And I know "it's been said many times, many ways" . . . but four months of Christmas music drives me insane.

We finish dinner, and Ricky goes off to his room to try to finish his homework in four minutes so that he can use his computer or watch television. Laurie and I linger over coffee. She likes coffee and I like delaying dealing with the discovery documents, so we can be here for a while.

The phone rings, and she looks at the caller ID. "Marcus."

It is perhaps the most ominous word in the English language, even though I don't think Marcus speaks the English language. Laurie answers, since she knows that she is the only one of us who understands what he says.

"Hello, Marcus," she says, and then listens for at least twenty seconds. Then, "Just Andy?"—which is as scary a question as I have ever heard. She listens for maybe ten seconds more. "You sure about this?"

This is getting worse all the time. I'm dying for her to get off the phone and tell me what is going on, and at the same time I am dreading her getting off the phone and telling me what is going on.

She finally hangs up. "You're not going to like this, and I certainly don't like it."

"I'm ready."

"Marcus says you can question Russell Estrada at eleven o'clock tonight in Eastside Park, down at the pavilion."

I look at my watch; it's only six thirty. "Is he with him now?"

"I don't think so. But I didn't ask the question."

"What else did he say?"

She shrugs. "Not much, except Marcus wants only you to come. Not me, Corey, or anyone else."

"Did he say why?"

"No. He said I should trust him, which of course I do. But I'm still not thrilled about it."

"I'm able to contain my enthusiasm as well. Did it sound like he was under any duress? Maybe they were forcing him to make the call?"

"Marcus?" She knows the question was ridiculous. "Marcus under duress? Someone forcing Marcus to do something?"

"Why would he not want you or Corey there? It doesn't make any sense."

"You'll find out at eleven o'clock, unless you decide not to go."

"I'll decide not to go fifty times between now and then, but you know I'll go. I have to."

"I can call him back and see what I can do to change the plan."

"No, I trust Marcus. But if he's not with Estrada now, he must be confident he can get his hands on him."

"Marcus has his ways."

I nod. "And they will be on display tonight."

Eastside Park is a ten-minute walk from my house.

I take Tara and Sebastian on a walk through this park at least once a day. I wish that's what I was doing now.

Tonight I'm not walking; I'm driving. By car it's about three minutes; which I am spending by trying not to throw up. I don't know exactly what I am going to find when I get to the pavilion at the lower level, but I'm quite certain I am going to be scared of it.

When I get the pavilion in sight, it's hard to make out anything that might be happening there. There's a little moonlight, but not much. Fortunately, it's unseasonably warm for this hour, maybe in the low forties. But the weather is not what I'm concerned about.

I park at the bottom of the hill, which is the closest I can get to the pavilion without driving across the baseball field. I get out of the car, which by itself takes a force of will I wasn't sure I possessed, and start walking toward the pavilion.

As I get closer, I can see that a car is there, and as I get closer still, I think it's Marcus's car. I don't see any people around, but it's possible that they are shielded by the car or are inside the car, or maybe they are inside the pavilion.

As I get closer, I see the figure of a man walking toward me. I can't see who it is, but I sure as hell hope it's Marcus. If it isn't, I am prepared to run. Feet, don't fail me now.

It's Marcus.

We meet up about seventy-five feet from the car and pavilion, and he says, "Ready." At least that's what I think he says.

"Is Estrada here?"

"Yunnh."

I take that as a yes. We walk toward the pavilion. Marcus walks faster than me because he's more anxious to get there than I am, and a couple of times he stops to let me catch up. When I finally get there, I see that a person I assume is Estrada is lying on his back. His hands are above his head, chained to a stone pillar, and his legs are about three feet from the car.

Fortunately, he's alive. I know that because he says, "Who the hell are you?"

I'm not inclined to answer that at the moment, especially since Marcus motions for me to walk over to the back of the car. When I do so, he pops the trunk. The light comes on, and I see to my horror that two large human beings are lying motionless in the trunk.

"Guards" is what I think he says, which I suppose means that they are, or were, Estrada's bodyguards. If that's the case, they seem to have been rather ineffective.

"Are they alive? Please tell me they're alive."

He nods. "Yunnh."

He walks back to Estrada; obviously I am here to

question him, and Marcus has placed him in answering mode. Marcus has obviously dismantled the threesome in a Marcus-style manner, which will hopefully induce cooperation.

"Why did you burn down Tony Birch's auto repair shop?" I ask.

"Who the hell is Tony Birch?"

"That is not going to make it any easier on you. You were rifling his desk and then you set fire to the place. We have your picture at the scene. So cut the bullshit and tell me why you did it."

"Kiss my ass."

Marcus walks to the car and picks something up that is attached to the rear right bumper. He then attaches it to something on Estrada's right leg. He starts to do something on the left side as well, and I suddenly realize why Marcus wanted me to come alone.

Laurie and Corey are both ex-cops. They believe in doing things by the book; threatening torture or actually torturing are not part of their repertoire. And killing is a major no-no. Marcus has his own way of doing things, and it is always effective. He's confident I won't interfere in a situation where Laurie or Corey would.

"Hey, what the hell are you doing?" Estrada asks, fear replacing bravado in his voice.

"It seems pretty obvious," I say, trying to control the tremor in my voice. "He's going to drive away and either the pillar, the bumper, or you are going to give way. You look like you're built pretty well; maybe it will turn out all right for you."

"Come on, he's crazy."

"You don't have to tell me that. But what you do have to tell me is why you burned down that shop."

"I didn't; I don't know what you're talking about."

It's understating the case to say that I am in a difficult spot here. I have never seen Marcus kill or even badly hurt someone unless he was defending himself or me or Laurie. I truly don't think he would brutally torture and kill Estrada, but the truth is that I can't be 100 percent sure. And if Marcus did do so, I would be legally culpable as well, which is not a minor consideration.

I'm sure that Estrada is a total scumbag, an arsonist, a thief, a drug dealer, and very possibly a murderer. But nobody deserves to die like this.

"You've got one more chance," I say.

"I don't know anything."

We've clearly reached an impasse, and the ball is in my court.

I trust Marcus.

"He's useless," I say to Marcus. "Do whatever you want." I try to make a facial expression to indicate that I am only saying this as a tactic, that I don't want him to do what we are threatening. But there is no way he can see that in the darkness.

I turn and walk away, back toward my car.

"Hey!" Estrada yells. "What the hell is going on?"

I don't stop or look back, though I am walking slowly. It's hard to walk fast and cringe at the same time. The next sound I hear is a car door opening; Marcus must be preparing to get in the car.

"Okay! Stop him! I'll tell you what I know!"

I stop and turn around. Marcus is standing by the open car door, watching me, as I walk toward Estrada.

"It's a pretty good bet that this is your last chance," I say.

"I torched the place."

"Why?"

"There was something in there that we didn't want found."

"Who is 'we'?"

"Me, and some people."

"What was it?"

"I don't know."

"Russell, Russell . . . you were doing so well there. Don't spoil it."

"I swear I don't know. Some kind of papers about . . ."

"About Luther?"

"Come on, man, he'll kill me."

"It seems like you're in more immediate jeopardy now. About Luther?"

Estrada pauses and decides to deal with his immediate problem. "Luther found out that Tony had something that could be dangerous to us. He got a phone call; I don't know from who. So he sent me over there."

"I'm going to need more from you, Russell."

"I swear, I've got nothing left."

I turn to Marcus. "We're back to square one." I turn to walk away again.

It's a wail coming from Tony: *"I swear!"*

I stop and walk back and whisper to Marcus, "Let them go."

He walks to the still-open trunk of the car, leans in, and takes the two large men out, one at a time. I think I see and hear them stirring, which pleases me greatly. "To paraphrase Hemingway, 'The young man opened the trunk; no thugs would die today.'"

Marcus lifts the two guys like they were five-pound bags of sand. He dumps them on the ground, then disconnects the chains from the bumper and from the pillar behind Estrada. Estrada is essentially free and unbound, yet he makes no effort to get up.

Marcus motions for me to get in the car, so I get in the passenger seat. He gets in as well and is obviously going to drive me to my car. It's a thirty-second ride, but it gives me a chance to ask the only question that matters.

"Marcus, would you have killed him?"

"Nnnhh."

That is Marcus-talk for "no." And right now, I think *nnnhh* may be the most beautiful word ever grunted.

As soon as I get home, I tell Laurie everything that happened in the park.

I'm still so stunned by the events that I'm shaking, and the wine is not helping. She doesn't say a word until I've completely finished.

"Now we know why Marcus didn't want me there."

I nod. "He only wanted someone who he was sure would not have the guts to stop it. What would you have done?"

"I would have stopped it. Not because I would have thought Marcus would have gone through with it; I know him better than that."

"He said afterwards that he wouldn't have done it."

She nods. "I'm not surprised, and I believe him. But I just don't think it's the right way to do things."

"Burning down a building, doing drugs, and committing violent crimes are not the right ways to do things either."

"I know that. But I like to maintain a distinction between those people and me. So what can you do with what you learned?"

It's the truth that I haven't even thought about it; I

was too busy being wrapped up and scared shitless by the evening's events. "I don't know yet. For one thing, it confirms what Chuck told me, which is no surprise. But it also shows that Luther has it in for Tony and is at least somewhat afraid of what Tony can do to him."

"But Tony doesn't know what that is," she says.

"That's what he says, anyway."

"You think he's lying?"

"It's possible," I say. "I don't see a logical way that Tony can have something so dangerous to Luther, yet not know what it is."

"So what's next?"

"We have to get to Luther. It may not yield anything . . . it probably won't . . . but we have to try. We're going into this trial unarmed. I'm afraid we have another job for Marcus."

"Corey and I are going to be there for this one."

"Marcus has already checked on Luther and knows where he does his business."

"He'll be well protected, especially after what happened to Estrada," she says.

"I would say there is a good chance Luther will never find out about what happened tonight. Estrada would be petrified for Luther to suspect that he told us anything, and the two bodyguards would not want him to know that they wound up unconscious in the back of a car."

"Maybe, maybe not," she says. "But he still won't be easy to get to."

"Marcus will figure out a way, but it might take some time."

"I'll get him started on it first thing in the morning."

It's only a half hour past midnight, which means it's only been an hour and a half since I arrived at the park pavilion. It feels like it's been a month.

I am not going to soon forget walking away, wondering if Marcus was going to get in that car and drive off, with Estrada attached to the bumper on one end and the pillar on the other.

So far this has not been a fun Christmas for Andy Carpenter, attorney-at-law.

The phone call shook Josh Winkler to his core.

It came to his office, and the first jolt came when the receptionist told him that "a friend of Luther is on the phone."

His first instinct was not to answer, to have her tell the caller that he was away or ill or dead. But he knew that would just be delaying the inevitable.

It was a voice he didn't recognize, which was no surprise since it had been years since his last involvement with these people. He had thought they were well in the rearview mirror, and he was intent on keeping it that way.

As soon as he picked up the phone, the caller said, "Luther wants to meet with you. Like the good old days."

The comment terrified Winkler, but he also found it strange. He and Luther had met only once, at the beginning of their "business" relationship. "What about?" he asked, though the answer wouldn't matter. He had no intention of ever having anything to do with Luther or his people ever again.

"He'll tell you that when you meet."

"I'm sorry, but I'm not interested. I've put all that be-hind me."

"It doesn't matter if you're interested. Luther wants to see you, so Luther will see you. You should know that by now."

"I'm sorry, I can't."

"You'll find a way. This is strictly business; no one is going to hurt you."

"Please."

The caller laughed a humorless laugh. "Be on the cor-ner of Fifty-first Street and Seventh Avenue, in front of the Michelangelo Hotel. A black SUV will pick you up at six thirty."

"Tell Luther I'm not interested in doing business."

"Tell him yourself."

Click.

Winkler hung up the dead phone and took some deep breaths, trying to think and compose himself. He had three options. One was to meet Luther and refuse his busi-ness offer. That presented an obvious danger; Luther was not the type to take rejection easily.

Another possible course of action would be to just not show up and maybe take an unscheduled vacation out of town. That might just be delaying the inevitable, al-though Luther might get the message and move on.

The third option would be to go to the police. That was the easiest one to reject. The caller, and Luther by extension, had done nothing illegal by merely asking for a meeting. Therefore the police could do nothing until something overt took place. But if Luther were to find out that Winkler went to the police, his life expectancy would take a sudden and precipitous drop.

Winkler instinctively felt that the first option was the smart way to go. Better to meet and get it over with. Once he found out what Luther wanted, he'd have a better sense of how to handle it. He was not going to get involved with Luther, that much was certain, but maybe he could finesse his way out. It all depended on what Luther had in mind.

But he was scared to go that route; the idea of meeting Luther was close to terrifying. So he spent the rest of the day contemplating his options. He had not carried a gun since that fateful day that the little girl was shot; he no longer even owned one. He regretted that now; it would have made him feel a little safer.

It wasn't until almost six o'clock that he decided he had to face whatever was confronting him. So he hopped in a cab and went to the address the caller had given. At six thirty, right on schedule, a black SUV pulled up.

"Get in the back." He did not recognize the driver, though his voice was clearly the same as the caller's.

Winkler climbed into the back and was surprised that no one else was in the car besides the driver. "Where is Luther?"

"We're going to see him now."

"What is this about?"

No answer from the driver; not that Winkler was expecting anything enlightening. The car headed uptown, taking city streets and then getting on the Westside Highway at Ninety-sixth Street. To Winkler's surprise, it got off at the exit for the George Washington Bridge and took the upper level into New Jersey.

"Where are we going?" he asked, but got no response.

The car got on to the Palisades Interstate Parkway North, past affluent New Jersey towns such as Englewood Cliffs and Alpine. Once it crossed back into New York State, it slowed at a rest stop, which was marked CLOSED and was blocked by a wooden barricade.

The driver was clearly not impressed by this and got off anyway, driving around the barricade and pulling around the small rest-stop building to the back.

Winkler was by now approaching full panic. Obviously no one else was around since the rest area was closed. And it was dark, with only a small amount of moonlight to see by.

"He's inside," the driver said.

That seemed strange to Winkler since no other cars were around and no light was coming from inside the building. Maybe Luther was dropped off there and would leave with the driver. But it didn't matter; Winkler was clearly at Luther's mercy with no way of escape.

He resolved in the moment to agree to any business relationship that Luther proposed. Anything to get out of here, to live another day.

Winkler opened the SUV door and started walking toward the rest-stop building. He did not hear any noise and wondered what he would find in there. Would it really be Luther? And if it was, why would he have arranged a meeting like this?

The three bullets that crashed into Winkler's back as he approached the door meant that he would never get the answer to those questions.

Ladies and gentlemen, I don't know any of you" is how Godfrey begins his opening to the jury.

"I know what you wrote on your questionnaires, and I heard your answers to the questions that Mr. Carpenter and I asked in voir dire, but I don't really know what makes you tick.

"Yet I feel very comfortable in saying that each of you has never done anything more important than the job you are undertaking starting today. It is as significant a task as any citizen can perform. You are the cogs that make our justice system run, and our justice system is crucial towards keeping this country great."

"But there is a difference between important and difficult. You must not allow the weight of responsibility to color your judgment or diminish your common sense. If you can do that, then your decision, while momentous, will be an easy one.

"Anthony Birch calmly laid in wait for Franklin Zimmer, hiding in the darkness and shooting him in the back of his head as he walked home one night on a street in downtown Paterson.

"He did the same to Raymond Hackett along a riverbank adjacent to a Newark park. The locations and victims were different, but the tactic was the same. Mr. Hackett was also shot in the head from behind.

"Both men were killed with the same gun, and we will clearly and beyond a shadow of a doubt connect that gun to Mr. Birch. And even though we are not required to demonstrate motive, in this case it is so obvious that it will be immediately clear to you.

"Neither Mr. Zimmer nor Mr. Hackett were what you would call fine, upstanding citizens. They had difficulties with law enforcement at times during their lives, and you would not approve of some of the things they had done.

"But they had paid their debts to society and were living as free men. They did not deserve to die. The law does not punish only those who murder the righteous.

"Anthony Birch cowardly and with intent murdered Franklin Zimmer and Raymond Hackett. It is our job to prove that beyond a reasonable doubt. Your job is to hold us to that obligation, and to vote to convict if we succeed.

"I am very confident that we will. Thank you."

Godfrey was effective; he commanded the room and had the jury hanging on every word. Of course, the trial just started; it will be a couple of days before their eyes start to glaze over.

He goes back to the prosecution table, sitting down next to the three other lawyers assisting on the case. Our table consists of me, Tony, and Eddie Dowd.

Judge Baron asks if I want to give my opening now or reserve it for the start of the defense case. As always, I opt to speak now.

"Ladies and gentlemen, it may surprise you to know that I agree with some of what Mr. Godfrey said. He is absolutely right when he says that your task is of immense importance, not only to the players in this case, but to society.

"You, and the citizens that preceded you in that jury box, and the ones that will succeed you, are the people that allow the system to function. And without a fair and impartial justice system, we would not recognize our country.

"I also agree with his description of the victims, Mr. Zimmer and Mr. Hackett. They were not choirboys; you would not approve of things they had done in their life. But as Mr. Godfrey said, they did not deserve to be gunned down.

"I'll even add something which might surprise you. My client, Anthony Birch, has also done things in his past that he is not proud of. He grew up on some pretty tough streets, with Mr. Zimmer and Mr. Hackett, and like them he took some wrong turns.

"But here's the difference. Mr. Birch turned his life around. He got a job, worked hard at it, and then started a business. He left that street life behind him and became the kind of citizen that we need in our community. He also left Mr. Zimmer and Mr. Hackett behind him; he had had no contact with them for years.

"The prosecution would have you believe that after all these years, Mr. Birch suddenly decided to throw away everything he had built and go on a murder spree. Then, after having years to plot his revenge, their position is that he nonetheless did it in such a stupid, obvious way that a child could piece the clues together.

"Quite simply, it makes no sense.

"Mr. Hackett and Mr. Zimmer dealt with some tough people in their lives, people who you will have no doubt are capable of murder. They are also people with a motive to have killed these two men, and the motive and opportunity to frame Mr. Birch.

"So, in one final area of agreement that I have with Mr. Godfrey, I ask that you bring your common sense with you to this courtroom every day.

"Thank you."

Michael Fales is Godfrey's first witness. He is the bartender at the Crown Bar that Laurie and I spoke to the day we visited the Zimmer crime scene. He was also working the night Zimmer was killed.

After establishing Fales's place of employment, Godfrey asks how long Fales has worked there. It's clearly an effort to show that Fales is a solid, reliable guy, because the answer is twenty-one years.

Godfrey establishes that Fales was working the night that Zimmer was killed. "Was the defendant, Anthony Birch, in the bar that night?"

"Yes."

Godfrey asks him to point to Tony to cement the identification, which Fales does, then asks him to describe Tony's interactions at the bar.

"He came in around eight o'clock and asked if Frankie Zimmer had been there. I said that he had not, and he shook his head, as if he was annoyed. I asked if he was expecting him, and he said yes."

"Had he ever been in the bar before?" Godfrey asks. "To your knowledge?"

"I can't say for sure, but I had never seen him in there. And I'm there almost every night."

"What about Mr. Zimmer? Had he ever been to your bar?"

"Oh, yeah. He was a regular. Maybe five or six nights a week."

"What did Mr. Birch do after you told him Mr. Zimmer was not there?"

"He asked for a beer and took a seat at a corner table. It was facing the door, and I noticed he was staring at that door the whole time he was there."

"How long did he stay?"

"Probably forty-five minutes. During that time he had three beers, then paid his bill and walked out."

"Was he angry?"

"He seemed it when I told him that Zimmer wasn't there. But I wasn't watching him the whole time; I was pretty busy."

"Did Mr. Zimmer ever show up that night?"

Fales nods. "Sure did. He got there maybe a half hour after Birch . . . the defendant . . . left. I told him that there had been someone looking for him, and he asked who it was. I described the guy, but I didn't know his name. I didn't think to look at the credit card receipt for the beers. Mr. Zimmer said he didn't know who it could have been, but he didn't seem that concerned about it."

Godfrey turns the witness over to me. Usually early witnesses like Fales are just scene setters, with the crucial stuff to come later. But in this case Fales has had some meaningful things to say: he identified Tony as being there that night and looking for the victim.

He has also left me an opening, which I need to exploit.

"Mr. Fales, you had no trouble identifying Mr. Birch a few minutes ago when Mr. Godfrey asked you to do so. Is that correct?"

"Yes."

"So Mr. Birch wasn't in disguise that night? He wasn't trying to conceal his identity?"

"No. Didn't seem like it."

"No fake mustache? Wig? Hoodie pulled down over his face?"

"No."

"And you said he paid with a credit card?"

"Yes."

"In his own name?"

"Yes."

"So just to be clear, he openly let you see his face and used a card which revealed his name. Is that correct?"

"Yes."

"And he also told you he was looking for Mr. Zimmer? And said that he was supposed to be meeting him there?"

"He said he was expecting Zimmer to be there."

"But Zimmer said the opposite, right? He didn't know of anyone that was supposed to be meeting him there?"

"That's right."

"When did you find out that Mr. Zimmer had been murdered that night?"

"Around noon the next day when I got in to work. The police were waiting for me at the bar."

"When they asked you if you had any idea who might have killed him, who was the first person you thought of to tell them?" I know the answer based on Fales's interview transcript, so I have no worries about asking the question.

"I think I told them about the defendant."

"He was your obvious suspect, right?"

"Seemed like it."

"Do you have any law enforcement experience? Did you ever work as a detective?"

"Nah."

"Yet you immediately identified Mr. Birch. He didn't exactly cover his tracks, did he?"

Godfrey objects and Judge Baron sustains.

"Let me put it this way. Did Mr. Birch do anything else that would have drawn attention to himself as a suspect?"

"Like what?"

"For example, did he wear a baseball cap with the word KILLER on it?"

Godfrey objects again and Judge Baron sustains. "Be careful, Mr. Carpenter."

"Yes, Your Honor. No further questions."

Next up is Ramiro Tejeda, and his being called answers a tactical question for me.

Rather than focus on one homicide at a time, Godfrey is going to present both cases simultaneously, bouncing back and forth between them. I think that is probably the right move, though he could risk confusing the jury. But he obviously thinks he has enough slam-dunk evidence to overcome that potential problem.

Godfrey wastes no time on Tejeda's background or occupation; he is there strictly to describe his actions on that specific day. Godfrey sets the scene and asks him what happened.

"Well, we were in Washington Park. They have an area where the dogs can run around and play with each other; it's fenced in. I take my dog there all the time. A lot of the people from our neighborhood do that."

"What kind of dog do you have?" Godfrey asks, smiling as if he gives a shit.

"A terrier mix. Her name is Ayla."

"Did something unusual happen that day?"

"Oh, yes."

"Please describe what happened."

"Well, one of the other people there that day was Dorina Mendoza. She has a beautiful dog named Chilly, very fast and powerful; he's a lot for her to handle. We always throw tennis balls, and the dogs chase them. Somebody threw a ball . . . I don't remember who . . . and it bounced over the fence. Dorina's dog jumped over that fence like it wasn't there and chased it."

"What did you do?"

"Well, Dorina started to scream because the ball was rolling towards the river next to the park. She was running after the dog, but of course she couldn't catch him. Me and a few of the other people started running as well, to help her if we could. But there was no way we were going to catch him, not the way he could run."

"What happened then?"

"Well, Chilly caught up to the ball, but then he dropped it. He started running down to the river. I was worried about him falling in."

"Did you catch up to him?" Godfrey asks.

"Yes, but only because he stopped running. We found him along the riverbank . . . digging at something. When we got there, we saw it was a dead body."

Tejeda is an example of a scene setter, someone who has information that is important to the prosecution in building their case, but whose testimony is uncontroversial and not able to be challenged.

Judge Baron asks if I have any questions for him, and I have only a couple.

"Mr. Tejeda, was the body hidden?"

"Not really. There were some leaves on it, I guess from the wind, but it was basically out in the open."

"Do people ever walk along that area?"

"Not really, but a bunch of people fish there. We had had some bad weather. But when it's sunny, there are definitely people there fishing."

"So if people were there fishing, they would have been likely to have seen the body?"

"Oh, yeah, it would be hard to miss it."

"Thank you. No further questions."

Judge Baron adjourns court for the day. The best I can say for it, the best I can say for most days when the prosecution is presenting their case, is that it wasn't awful. It's rare that the defense has a huge day just on cross-examinations; it's hard to score big points when playing defense. As Eddie would say, there are few pick-sixes in a jury trial.

Today's witnesses have not been terribly damaging; those are soon to follow.

I say good-bye to Tony, and Eddie and I head for the exit. I'm surprised to see Laurie there waiting for us.

"Anything wrong?" I ask.

"Josh Winkler was found dead this morning at a rest stop on the Palisades Interstate."

"Damn. Any witnesses or suspects?"

"I don't think so. Corey is checking with some contacts."

"Luther," I say.

There is a definite chance that I killed Josh Winkler.

Depending on how this plays out, we could find that my bringing him into the case stirred up something that resulted in his death. He'd had no contact with Luther for years, until Andy Carpenter blundered into his office and placed him in danger.

But if that is the case, it raises a basic question. How would Luther or anyone else have known that I met with Winkler at all? Was he being watched? Am I being followed? Did he share the fact of our meeting with anyone?

And what about our meeting could have prompted his murder? It was a fairly uneventful conversation and centered more on his actions than anyone else's. Yes, he admitted that Luther was his drug connection back in those days, but he only told me that to avoid its coming out publicly. He clearly announced he had no interest in reliving those days and certainly did not seem like a threat to anyone.

I can hope that my intervention was not the cause. Luther seems to be on a crusade to clean things up, attempting to violently erase some history that seems a danger to him. Winkler could just have been another unfortunate victim of that spree.

To make matters worse, Sam calls and starts the conversation off in a decidedly unpromising way. "I've run into two dead ends."

"Wonderful. Let's hear it."

"I was trying to trace the burner phone that called Tony that day. I was hoping I could show that Zimmer bought it. But it was paid for in cash at a convenience store."

"And the other dead end?"

"I keep trying to find Richie Sanford, the brother of that little girl. But no luck; he's completely off the grid. I've tried everything."

It's rare that Sam can't deliver on something I ask for, and I know how much it bothers him. "Not your fault, Sam. Thanks."

Laurie sets up a meeting at the house with Marcus and Corey to discuss Marcus's plan for meeting up with Luther. She has set it up for 9:00 P.M.; we could have done it earlier, but Ricky will be in bed by then. These are the kinds of meetings that child psychologists would probably recommend that eleven-year-old boys not attend.

I haven't been spending much time with him; which represents a major reason that I want to retire. But the little time I do get to be with him during a trial centers me and helps me understand what is important.

Tonight I take him on my nightly walk with Tara and Sebastian through Eastside Park. We talk mostly about football; it's a measure of how tied up I am with the case that I haven't focused on it much.

"Dad, are the Giants ever going to make the playoffs?"

he asks. As has happened for far too many years in a row, this year they haven't come close.

"Someday," I say. "Things change. You know they've won four Super Bowls, right?"

He frowns. "Yeah, but the last one was when I was two years old. I don't think I remember it."

"I'll tell you what. The next time they are in the play-offs, we'll go to the games."

"Really?"

"Absolutely. And your wife can come too."

He laughs. Laurie and I adopted Ricky, but somehow he inherited her great laugh. Their laughs light up every room they are in, even an outdoor one as big as this park.

When we get back, we play a game of *Madden* football on his Xbox. The new version is one of the gifts Laurie picked out for Ricky for Christmas. I do much better than usual; I lose 35–14. Ricky is great at it; I have a hunch that he does not spend all the time he's in his room doing homework.

I tuck him into bed and then leave his room and reenter the real world, the one in which we are going to deal with a vicious gang leader. Marcus and Corey show up at nine o'clock. Corey brings Simon Garfunkel to play with Tara; Simon may well have a role to play in the operation, but he doesn't need to hear the details now.

Mercifully, Laurie has gone over the plans with Marcus earlier in the day, so she is able to lay it out for us.

"As you've heard before, Luther works out of three different offices, in Passaic, Newark, and Elizabeth. He's most often in Passaic, but it's fairly random, and there is no sure way to predict where he will be on a given night.

He is also always well protected by multiple bodyguards at each place, and the locations are set up so that there is no way to sneak up on them.

"But he is not a night owl; he usually heads home by ten o'clock. Sometimes he brings a woman with him, but usually not. He always has at least two bodyguards with him."

"So where do we meet up with him?"

"At his house. There are always one or two bodyguards there, keeping the house secure, even when Luther is not there. Marcus thinks we should be there as a welcoming party when he gets home. Luther has apparently gotten comfortable living the suburban life, and Marcus thinks he's more likely to let down his guard there than on the city streets where his offices are."

According to Laurie, Marcus hasn't noticed any increased security, which confirms for me my hunch that Estrada and his bodyguards would not share the story of their Eastside Park interaction with Marcus and me the other night. I'm not surprised; if Luther thought that Estrada gave us information or even knew how easily we subdued them, it would likely not go well for any of them.

Laurie shows us photographs of the estate from various angles. Marcus has done a remarkable job planning the operation. It's a sign that he is taking it seriously, which by definition means a significant challenge is ahead of us.

Not surprisingly, I have no role to play other than to hang around until we have achieved success. Then I will be the one to question Luther, which I have to admit I am not looking forward to.

"When do we do this?" I ask, hoping that the answer will be August.

"Tomorrow night," Laurie says. "Right, Marcus?"

"Yunnh."

We'll just have to leave it at that.

Whenever there are multiple murders, chances often are that some are a smoke screen. It's possible that is the case here, but I'm not seeing it yet.

There is no shortage of bodies "lying around" in this case. Frankie Zimmer and Raymond Hackett are local. Josh Winkler and the broadcaster Terry Banner represent the out-of-town deceased contingent. We could also throw in TJ Richardson, who was killed in prison while he served time for shooting the Sanford child.

Both Banner and Winkler could conceivably fit the bill as the primary target, although Banner is the more likely candidate. Since great effort has apparently been put into making Tony the fall guy, the Winkler murder does not seem to fit. Even Godfrey wouldn't contend that Tony managed to kill him while he was in prison and on trial.

It's going to be difficult to concentrate in court today. I'll have to use mental gymnastics not to be looking ahead to our planned adventure with Luther tonight. I'm better at mental than physical gymnastics, but it's still going to take a major effort.

Godfrey's first witness is Sergeant Thomas Fanning of

the Paterson Police Department. He works homicide under Pete Stanton, though Lieutenant James Lavalle is the
officer he reported to on this case. Fanning was the first to
reach the scene on Bergen Street the night that Zimmer's
body was discovered.

Godfrey has him discuss what he did that night.

"By the time we got there, a small crowd had formed.
It was late, so there weren't as many people as would have
been there earlier. And it's not a residential neighborhood."

"What did you do first?"

"My partner moved the people back and secured a pe-
rimeter. I went to the victim and determined that he was
deceased. At that point I called both the paramedics and
the coroner, as well as Homicide and Forensics."

"Where was the body?"

"On the sidewalk, but wedged against a wall. It seemed
likely that he was shot while walking, and the impact sent
him sideways. It was dark, so it was difficult to see him
in the shadows."

"Were you able to determine where the bullet came
from?"

"That came later. All I could see was that he was shot
in the back of the head. It was obviously a catastrophic
wound."

"What did you do next?"

"We set out to interview everyone present in the hope
that someone saw something that would be helpful."

"And did they?"

Sergeant Fanning shakes his head. "No. Or at least
they all claimed they did not. It's impossible to know if

someone saw something but did not want to get involved. That's a fairly tough area."

Godfrey turns him over to me. Fanning simply told the factual truth, and it did not incriminate Tony, so there is little to get from him. Having said that, I always like to make at least some point with every witness, just to keep the jury on its toes.

"Sergeant Fanning, you said the place where the shot was fired from was discovered later. Can you tell us where that was, if you know?"

"Yes, there was a crevice, almost like an inset between two stores. The shooter was in there; it would have been too dark to have seen him."

"So is it fair to say that your theory would be that the shooter waited there until Zimmer came by on his way home, then once he passed him, the shooter came out, fired, and left the scene?"

"Yes, that is how I saw it."

That is a mistake by Fanning; it is not his job to entertain such theories, and he should have declined to answer my question. I take out a large street map of the area and introduce it as evidence.

We have highlighted the Crown Bar, where Zimmer began his fateful walk, as well as Zimmer's home, close to a mile away, and the spot where the shooting occurred. Fanning confirms that the map is accurate.

"Here's the route that Mr. Zimmer was taking. It measures at one and one eighth miles. Here's another possible route." I draw it on the map with a Sharpie. "It measures out at a mile and a quarter, slightly longer."

Then I take the Sharpie and draw another possible

route. "This one measures at nine tenths of a mile, slightly shorter than the route Mr. Zimmer chose. So my question is, if the shooter was going to lie in wait for his victim, how would he know which route that victim would take?"

"Objection," Godfrey says. "This is outside the scope of the direct testimony."

"Your Honor," I say, "the witness opened the door by advancing his own theory as to where the shooter waited and how he committed the act. I am clearly entitled to challenge that."

"Objection overruled," Judge Baron says. "The witness will answer the question."

Fanning immediately looks worried; he realizes he blundered in opening the door by advancing his theory. He asks me to repeat the question, which I do. His answer is "Hard to say, maybe he was willing to not kill him that night, but wait for another night if he guessed the wrong route."

"Here's another theory; tell me if it's possible. This hypothetical is that there was more than one perpetrator involved, and each was covering a different route. That way they would be sure to encounter Mr. Zimmer that night. Is that possible?"

"There's no evidence of that," Fanning says.

"Is there evidence to prove it wrong, beyond a reasonable doubt?"

"I don't know."

"Of course you don't. There's no way anyone could. No further questions."

Sticking with his tactic of switching back and forth between the two homicides, Godfrey calls Sergeant Michael

Escalante, the first cop on the scene at the discovery of Raymond Hackett's body in the Newark park.

Godfrey's direct examination is surprisingly perfunctory; he is suddenly controlling his desire to overtalk everything. He merely has Escalante describe the scene when he arrived at the riverbank, including the location of the bullet wound and the condition of the body.

I start what will be a brief cross-examination. "Sergeant Escalante, you said there was one bullet wound in the back of the head?"

"That's all I saw. You could check the autopsy."

"I have, thank you. Are there generally people in that area of the park during the day?"

"Yes, it's a popular place since they redid it. Even when it snows, kids play there, and people bring their dogs."

"What about at night?"

"I've never been there at night, but it closes at eight P.M., so there shouldn't be anyone."

"So if a murder was committed there, using a firearm, it would attract a great deal of attention during the day, but possibly none at night?"

He nods. "Makes sense."

"So here's a hypothetical that I'd like you to think about. Since no one goes in that park at night, and there is certainly no fishing at that time, the victim, Raymond Hackett, was probably not just walking along the riverbank when he ran into his murderer. Do we agree so far?"

"Makes sense." Escalante is probably driving Godfrey crazy.

"I agree. So that would mean that the chances are that his murderer met him elsewhere and took him to that riverbank, where he killed him. That way no one could have seen him commit the murder."

Godfrey objects that I am testifying rather than questioning the witness. I push back, saying that I am merely presenting a hypothetical that the witness can agree with or not. Judge Baron overrules the objection, which pleases and surprises me.

Escalante agrees that it's certainly possible, and even likely, that the killer and his victim met elsewhere and then came to the riverbank.

"In this hypothetical, why would the killer have had to shoot him in the back of the head?" I ask.

Escalante thinks about it for a few moments. "I don't know, maybe he just wanted to? Maybe he didn't want the victim to know what was coming?"

"Could it be that he wanted it to look like the same as the Zimmer killing? To make it obvious that the same person committed both crimes?"

Godfrey objects again, and this time Judge Baron sustains. I withdraw the question and let Escalante off the stand. Godfrey was right; I was testifying, and I think I did a damn good job, if I do say so myself.

'm not sure my law school professors would have approved of my participating in a home invasion. I can't be sure because it never came up in class. But I just sense that they would have frowned on it.

As former cops, I doubt that Laurie and Corey are too thrilled about it either, but they have agreed to be willing participants. I think they are doing so to make sure things go well, to protect me, and to prevent any unnecessary violence. My telling them about the events in Eastside Park with Russell Estrada and Marcus has them worried.

All of us, other than Marcus, drive there in Corey's car. Corey drives, with Laurie in the passenger seat and Simon Garfunkel and me in the backseat. Simon rests his head on my lap while I pet him; if he's nervous, he's hiding it well.

The plan is for us to wait in a grammar school parking lot, less than five minutes from Luther's home. Marcus will call us when he's ready for us. We arrive at nine o'clock, and fifteen minutes later Laurie's cell phone rings. It's Marcus, telling us to move in.

We make the short drive to Luther's house. It's secluded

and at the top of a hill. He probably chose this place for the protection that the location afforded him, but it works well for our purposes tonight.

We know our way around because of the photos Marcus had provided. We park back behind the house, near the swimming pool, so that Luther will not be able to see our car as he approaches.

Our first surprise as we arrive is revealed by our car lights just before we stop. Two large people are lying on their backs, with their hands tied to the railing on the steps leading into the pool. There are also gags on their mouths. I have no idea as to the procedure Marcus employed to neutralize them; he didn't seek my counsel beforehand.

They turn their heads to see us pull up, which is a pretty good indication that they are alive. That is a relief.

Marcus comes casually out to greet us, like the lord of the manor. He looks so at home that I half expect him to ask us what we'd like to drink.

"Any trouble?" Laurie asks, though the sight of the two disabled bodyguards pretty much answers the question already.

"Nnnhh," Marcus says.

We take our positions. Mine is behind a large tree. It will conceal me while allowing me a view of the front of the house, which is where the action will take place.

Marcus goes into the house as Laurie and Corey conceal themselves along the sides. Corey has Simon with him; hopefully Simon has more barking discipline than Tara would show when a car pulls up to the house.

At ten after ten, the car arrives. From my vantage point it looks like two men are in the front seat, and one in the back. I've seen photographs of Luther, but in this light I can't tell which one is him.

Marcus wasn't sure if the bodyguards enter the house and stay there all night, or if they just drop Luther off. He suspects the latter, since there are already two guards in the house. Of course, in this case they are incapacitated out by the pool, but the arriving threesome has no way of knowing that.

All three men get out of the car and start walking toward the house. The two guards walk about two feet ahead of Luther, who I can see fairly clearly now. It's possible that they are just making sure he gets into the house safely before they depart. It doesn't matter what their intentions are.

They are about to receive a surprise.

As one of the guards reaches for the doorknob, the entire door crashes outward, as if it exploded from the house. Marcus had taken it off its hinges, so he has not technically broken down the door.

But that is a distinction without a difference. The door hits the two guards, sending them to the ground. Luther is far back enough to be able to get out of the way, but that is fine for our purposes. Laurie and Corey move in, guns drawn, and Marcus comes out of the house. Marcus didn't bring a gun; or if he did, he's not showing it. He just brought Marcus, which is plenty.

Simon's job is to hang around looking scary, and he performs his task with great professionalism. He snarls at the guards on the ground, as if he is about to tear them apart. It's an amazing transformation from the dog that accepted petting from me on the way here.

Laurie and Marcus take the two bodyguards to the back of the house, where they will join their two friends. Corey instructs Luther to move toward a bench on the side of the house. I'm not sure if it's Corey's gun or Simon that Luther is more afraid of, but he does as he's told.

I had felt that we should conduct the questioning outdoors in the dark; it might be more disconcerting for Luther. The others agreed, probably to humor me, which is why we're doing it out here, on the bench.

The sad fact is that I'm not expecting to get any real information out of Luther; I am looking more for reactions.

"Who the hell are you?" Luther asks, starting the conversational ball rolling.

"Your worst nightmare," I say. It's a line from one of the thirty-eight *Rambo* movies that I've always wanted to use. I think I can tell in the darkness that Corey is frowning at me. "Now, why did you kill Josh Winkler?"

"Who?" Luther asks.

"Josh Winkler."

"After all this you came to the wrong place. I never heard of that guy."

The way he said it makes me think he might be telling the truth. "You used to do business with him. You sent somebody to shake him down a long time ago and a little girl got killed."

"Right . . . I remember that. He's dead?"

"You killed him."

"Bullshit. We haven't dealt with him in years."

"What about Tony Birch?"

He snorts derisively. "That piece of shit."

"You had your flunky Estrada burn down his business."

"If he wasn't in jail, I'd have killed him. So I did the next best thing and burned down his place. That's just for now . . . when he's serving time in Rahway, his ass will be mine."

"Why?"

"He was going to turn on me. He had tapes from dealing with my people. He was going to use it to make a deal on the murder charges."

"You set him up on those charges. You killed Zimmer and Hackett and planted the gun at Birch's house."

"You don't know what the hell you are talking about. Why would I kill those guys? And if I wanted Birch out of the way, he'd be out of the way."

He's asking questions that I cannot answer, questions I've asked myself. I think he's lying . . . he must be lying . . . but he's doing a good job of it.

"Estrada is going down for arson."

He laughs. "Yeah? We'll see about that." Then, "I heard what happened in the park the other night. Was that you?"

"We are everywhere. And you're going to tell us what we want to know or you are not going to live to see tomorrow." It's a line that defines the term *empty threat*.

"Kiss my ass." It's possible I haven't fully intimidated him.

Laurie and Marcus come from behind the house to join us. "How's it going?" Laurie asks.

"We're done here," I say.

"You're done, all right," Luther says. "Do you have any idea who you just messed with?"

Corey speaks for the first time. "Yeah, a tough, scary guy. Just keep in mind that four bodyguards couldn't protect you. We can get to you whenever we want, you little punk. And if we come back, it won't be to ask questions."

Russell Estrada was trying to maintain a business-as-usual approach. There was plenty to be done running his portion of Luther's operation, and he attacked it full-time. It kept his mind off the other night.

In the four days since that night in Eastside Park, Estrada had been worried that Luther would find out what had happened. He secured the promise of the two bodyguards with him that night not to say anything, but he couldn't be sure that they would keep their word. But since they hadn't covered themselves with glory either and spent the crucial time unconscious in the trunk, it was likely that they'd be okay keeping their mouths shut.

What Russell was not aware of was that one of the guards, while not telling Luther, had shared the news with another member of the gang. That person went directly to Luther with the information, as a way to curry favor.

In any event, Luther had not acted any differently toward Estrada since that night, and Luther was not inclined to be subtle. If he thought for a moment that Estrada had given up any information dangerous to him, Luther would immediately have acted to make Estrada regret his actions. No one had to tell Estrada how ruthless Luther could be; Estrada had seen it firsthand many times and had often done Luther's dirty work for him.

Luther and Estrada had been together at the Passaic office this evening. It was two rooms behind a bar that Luther owned. Nothing glamorous, but the location and setup made it easy to defend and fortify. That was important, even though it had been a long time since anyone had challenged Luther or the Blood Dragons.

Luther left at around nine thirty, which had become standard for him for at least a year. At that hour Estrada's night was just beginning: there were collections to be handled, drops to be made, discipline to be handed out.

So with the same two bodyguards who were with him that night in the park, Estrada set out at around eleven thirty to make his rounds. The first stop was in Paterson. It was a weekly collection from their people in charge of the drug and prostitution ring in that city. Those people were reliable; they always took their allowed cut and handed over the bulk of the money, as agreed.

That night was no different. They met in an alley off Market Street, same as always. The handoff was uneventful, and few words were spoken. Everything as usual.

The only departure from normal was the semiautomatic fire that gunned down Russell Estrada and his two bodyguards as they were getting into their car.

It's just a little over twenty miles from Paterson to New York City. So even though Paterson is a relatively large city of 145,000 people, it is still basically a New York suburb. When people in and around Paterson refer to "the city," they are talking about New York.

One of the obvious examples of that is the television stations we get. We receive the broadcasts from the New York network affiliates and independent stations; when we turn on the local news, it covers the entire metropolitan area, which has New York as its center.

Therefore news from Paterson rarely makes it on the air. There are just too many things to compete with, and the truth is that it would take a relatively momentous Paterson event to make someone in Manhattan or Queens or Long Island care enough to watch.

But when Laurie and I wake up this morning and turn on the television, Paterson is front and center. That's because of the triple murder on a Paterson street last night. And we are especially interested in it because the victims are Russell Estrada and his two bodyguards, the same three people that Marcus and I had spent time with during our adventure in Eastside Park the other night.

According to the reports, the shootings happened around midnight, close to an hour and a half after we left Luther's house.

"Do you think we set it in motion?" Laurie asks.

"It's a coincidence if we didn't," I say. Neither Laurie nor I have ever believed in coincidences, and that we both feel the same way about it is no coincidence.

"Did you talk about Estrada?" Laurie had been behind the house with Marcus, making sure the bodyguards were incapable of interfering with us.

I nod. "Some. I told him that Estrada was going down for arson."

"What did he say?"

"He laughed and said something like 'we'll see about that.' I thought it was bluster, or that he meant Estrada would somehow beat the rap. He could have meant that Estrada would be too dead to stand trial. But he somehow knew about what happened in the park; he brought it up."

"This happened awful fast," Laurie says. "Luther would have had to give the order almost as soon as we left."

"All it would take would be one phone call."

"If it wasn't us, then he found out about the night in the park some other way. If one of the bodyguards, or even Estrada himself, told Luther, then they made a serious misjudgment."

We watch for any updates, then I quickly shower, get dressed, and take Tara and Sebastian on their morning walk. I am certainly not mourning the loss of Estrada and the two others; they most likely have done things that warranted that punishment. I don't like the way it was handed out, but there are greater tragedies in the world.

If we spurred Luther into violent retribution last night, it was pretty much the only thing we accomplished. I was hoping to detect reactions that would be revealing, but I don't really think I did.

He seemed sincere in not knowing about Josh Winkler's death, and that was supported by his openly talking about his dislike for Tony Birch and the reason he burned down his business. But he could just as easily have been lying about Winkler's murder. He remains in my mind the only suspect, since Winkler seemed to have put the drug life behind him and would therefore seem an unlikely candidate for such a violent death at the hands of anyone else.

I make it to court with just ten minutes to spare. Last night was that rare time during a trial that I didn't spend in preparation for the next day's witnesses; instead I spent it executing a home invasion on a gang leader. Assuming Godfrey didn't do the same, he'll have an advantage on me.

Tony has heard about the Estrada murder, and he asks me about it when he sits down next to me at the defense table. "Does it have anything to do with our case?"

I shrug. "I don't know, but I'm starting to think that everything that happens in the world is tied to our case."

Godfrey's first witness of the day is Sergeant Nate Kroeger. He works in the Forensics Division of the Paterson Police Department, and he has an easy job today. Godfrey has already informed the court that Kroeger will be testifying twice, and this first round is to discuss completely noncontroversial stuff, although I will do my best to make it seem otherwise.

I have stipulated that Kroeger can testify about both murder scenes, even though he did not actually work the Newark murder. He's gone over the reports and consulted with the Newark forensics people; I gain nothing by forcing Godfrey to put two different people on the stand.

Once he's established Kroeger's credentials and swooned over his thirty years in the business, Godfrey asks, "Sergeant Kroeger, can you please talk about any similarities you found between the two scenes?"

Kroeger pauses as if absorbing the question, even though there is no question that all of this has been rehearsed. "Well, for one thing, both victims were shot in the back of the head, with a .38-caliber revolver. For another, each was shot from a distance, between eight and twelve feet."

"Would you consider that a difficult shot?"

"With that weapon and the fact that at least one of the shootings was done at night with a moving target? Absolutely."

Godfrey introduces as evidence Tony's records from a local shooting range. Unfortunately, Tony is an accomplished marksman, or at least he was back in the day.

"Any other similarities?" Godfrey asks.

Kroeger nods. "Most importantly, the same gun was used in both instances."

"Are you certain of that?"

"Positively, without question."

Godfrey asks a few more questions that basically cover

the same ground, and he has Kroeger discuss the technical ballistics aspects. Kroeger's testimony is not damaging yet; the crusher will come when they tie the gun to Tony.

My cross starts with "Sergeant Kroeger, have you ever fired a similar weapon?"

"Yes, I have."

"In competition?" I know the answer to every question I'm asking because Eddie Dowd has dug up the information.

"Yes."

"Are you a champion? Do you often win those competitions?"

"Not really. I've won a couple, but I'm basically in the middle of the pack."

"How big are the packs, generally?"

"Probably anywhere between fifty and a hundred shooters, depending."

"Always the same people?"

"No. Depends where the competition is held."

"So over the course of, say, the last five years, you might have competed against close to a thousand people? I actually have the records if you need them to refresh your recollection."

"That sounds about right."

"And there are competitions that you don't enter?"

"Of course."

"Could you make the shots that we're talking about in this case? Hitting someone in the head at eight to twelve feet?" I'm sure he wants to say no, but I'm hoping that the truth and his ego will prevent that.

"Yes." Then he smiles. "But I wouldn't."

I return the smile. "Since you described yourself as being in the middle of a pack of a thousand people, and you could make that shot, is it fair to say that most of those people could also do it?"

"I think so."

"Me too," I say. "No further questions."

The next witness is going to do tremendous damage to our case.

There is no way of getting around that. It will be my job to try to keep it from being a disaster, but it will be a heavy lift.

Cynthia Daughtrey was a court clerk in the Passaic County Courthouse for more than thirty years. She retired about two years ago, and if there is anyone who dealt with her during her tenure who did not like her, I haven't run into them.

Godfrey takes her through her career path. It wasn't exactly a winding one; she got the job in Passaic County and stuck with it for her entire career. Godfrey gets her to reluctantly admit that she never took a sick day, not a single one in all those decades.

The problem for me, and certainly for Tony, is that she is instantly likable and believable. She also has the advantage of actually telling the truth.

"Were you the court clerk during a legal matter involving the defendant six years ago?"

"Yes, I was."

Godfrey has to be careful here. The crime that Tony was on trial for, involuntary manslaughter, is not admissible before this jury unless the defense brings it in. If Godfrey mistakenly does so, it could be grounds for a mistrial.

"Do you remember Franklin Zimmer, one of the murder victims in this case, testifying during that trial?"

"I do."

Godfrey feigns being amused. "Do you remember every witness in every trial you were at over the course of your thirty years?"

"Oh, goodness no."

"Is there a particular reason you remember that one?"

She nods. "When Mr. Zimmer left the stand, he walked towards the gallery, and he passed within maybe ten feet of Mr. Birch. Mr. Birch stood up and screamed at him."

"What did he say?"

"Well, I'm not sure I remember all of the exact words, and there was some profanity, but he definitely said he was going to kill him, that he would 'tear his heart out.' The bailiffs restrained him, although he didn't really seem to make a move toward Mr. Zimmer."

"Did I ask you to go over the transcript of that trial in preparation for your testimony here today?" Godfrey asks.

"Yes. I did so."

"Was Raymond Hackett, the other victim in this case, also a witness in that trial?"

"Yes, sir."

"As you read the transcript, did he also testify against Mr. Birch's interests?"

"He did."

There is almost nothing for me to do with this.

Daughtrey has clearly demonstrated a motive; there is no talking my way out of that.

I start with "Ms. Daughtrey, having spent all of those years being present at court trials, you must be familiar with these kind of things . . . emotional outbursts?"

"Yes."

"Trials can be intense, can they not? With so much at stake?"

She nods. "Absolutely."

"And when something like you described happens, you're more likely to remember that, aren't you?"

"Of course."

"Everyone present would be likely to remember it, wouldn't they? It was the kind of thing that you don't see every day."

"I would certainly agree with that."

"So Mr. Birch would have known that an entire courtroom full of people . . . the judge, the jury, the lawyers, the court clerk, the spectators . . . all of them would have seen the threat, and they'd likely remember it for years?"

"I would think so."

"And some of those people would also remember Mr. Hackett's testimony?"

"Not as many, but some," she says.

"But of course it's in the transcript, there for the authorities to see."

"Yes."

"It made perfect sense to you that the police would have looked at Mr. Birch for this crime, didn't it?"

"I suppose so."

"And the fact that both men were murdered within

such a short time, in the same manner, after six years, makes it even more obvious, correct?"

"Yes, I would say so."

"Almost too obvious?"

Godfrey objects, and Judge Baron sustains.

I try and rephrase in a way that will get the point across clearly. "If the prosecution is right, and Mr. Birch committed these two murders, would you say, based on your experience, that he did it in a way likely to call attention to himself?"

Godfrey objects again, but Judge Baron lets her answer.

"I certainly would."

The prosecution will be wrapping up its case in the next day or two. That's the good news. The bad news is that we will have to then present our case. Good luck with that.

We have a villain in the person of Luther. He touches every aspect of the case, and every tentacle leading off of it. He is connected to everyone that has been killed, and the list is long. Richardson, Zimmer, Hackett, Estrada and his two bodyguards, Winkler, even Banner, the newscaster in Scranton.

What I don't understand, or perhaps I should say what is at the top of the long list of things I don't understand, is why Tony is alive. Why would Luther have killed everyone else, but chosen to frame Tony? If Tony had something that was dangerous to him, and Luther obviously thought he did, wouldn't that make him the first one to be killed? Going to prison would not stop him from talking nearly as effectively as a bullet in the head.

I believe that Luther is behind everything. My view is that if the jury were to learn what I know, then they would consider it reasonable to at least think of Luther as a suspect. And by definition that would mean reasonable doubt as to Tony's guilt.

The problem is I don't know how the hell to get the jury to know what I know. There is no obvious connection to link people like Winkler and Banner and even Estrada to this case. And there is no reason I can point to for Luther to have wanted Zimmer and Hackett dead. Tony's motive for killing them, as testified to by Daughtrey, is obvious. Luther's, not so much.

I seem to bring death and destruction wherever I go. I talked to Winkler and he's dead. I talked to Estrada, and he and the two bodyguards are dead. I took on Tony as a client, and his shop got burned to the ground. I'm a real good-luck charm.

There has to be more going on than just an effort to frame Tony. A number of these killings, including those of Winkler, Estrada, and the bodyguards, took place after Tony was arrested. I know they must all be connected, but I don't know how.

Unfortunately, I don't have a lot of time to figure it out.

Godfrey's first witness this morning is a recall of Nate Kroeger, the Paterson forensic cop. This time he's bringing far more serious weapons to attack our case.

"Sergeant Kroeger, were you there the day that a search, pursuant to a legal warrant, was conducted on Mr. Birch's house?"

"I was."

"Are you aware that a gun was found buried in his backyard?"

"Yes."

"Did you examine that gun?"

"I did. It was a .38-caliber revolver."

"Was that the same .38-caliber revolver that fired the bullets that killed Franklin Zimmer and Raymond Hackett?"

"Definitely."

Godfrey takes Kroeger through a five-minute, boring lecture on ballistics, to demonstrate why he is certain that this was the gun.

"Was there anything else found buried with the gun?"

"Yes. A white handkerchief."

"Did you examine the handkerchief for DNA?"

"Yes. There was DNA from two people detected. By far the most DNA belonged to Mr. Birch. There was a small amount of trace DNA from someone else that we were not able to identify."

The jury has clearly been hanging on every word that Kroeger is saying; that the murder weapon was found buried on Tony's property is stunning, even though they probably knew it was coming.

For the first time in the trial, I let a witness off the stand without asking questions. On the one hand I want it to seem like I don't consider this a big deal, but the truth is I want to save my ammunition for when Lieutenant James Lavalle gets on the stand to tie up the loose ends of Godfrey's case.

Godfrey seems intent on stretching things out and delaying that confrontation. He calls three witnesses, all of whom were former members of the Fulton Street Boyz, the gang that Tony, Zimmer, and Hackett were members of.

He would claim to be explaining the history of the

relationships between the three men, but what he is really doing is exposing Tony's gang history.

I am torn here. On the one hand I want to ask questions forcing these guys to talk about Luther and the Blood Dragons. On the other hand, Tony would automatically be implicated in that violent world. I'll hold off for now, but I might decide I have to take the risk in our case.

We're nearing the end of the day, so Judge Baron adjourns early. Lieutenant Lavalle will be the star witness tomorrow.

I'm surprised when Godfrey doesn't start the day with Lavalle.

Instead he calls Dr. Todd Castleman, who works in the Jersey State Laboratory. Castleman had been on the witness list, but I just assumed that Godfrey decided he wasn't necessary. That would have made sense because he certainly isn't necessary.

Castleman is on the stand to beat home the DNA science. He is focused on the handkerchief, and the possibility that it is not Tony's DNA. The chance of a misidentification, according to Castleman, is one in many, many billions.

I don't think the jury doubted the results before, so I don't think they needed Castleman to convince them. But Godfrey obviously thinks it is important enough to have it pounded into their heads.

I have no intention of trying to find a flaw in the DNA, especially since I have no interest in claiming that it's not Tony's handkerchief. I view the handkerchief as a plus for us, rather than a minus, but I'm not going to reveal that now.

I just have one thing to focus on. "Dr. Castleman, you've testified that there was also some trace DNA on the handkerchief that did not belong to Mr. Birch, is that correct?"

"Yes."

"Did you try and learn whose DNA that was?"

"Yes, but without success. It was not in any of the data banks we use."

"Is it possible that this other person put the handkerchief in the ground along with the gun?"

"I have no idea."

"You have no idea if it's even possible?"

"Well, anything is possible."

I let him off with that, and Godfrey finally calls Lieutenant James Lavalle, of the Paterson PD, Homicide Division. Pete Stanton has often told me how good Lavalle is, so I am looking forward to the challenge.

Godfrey establishes Lavalle's credentials, which are considerable. Then, "You were in charge of this case from the beginning?"

"The Zimmer homicide, yes. The Hackett homicide was investigated by Newark PD, but once it became obvious that the two cases were connected, we collaborated. Since Mr. Birch was already in custody here, they agreed that we should take the lead role."

"So you're fully versed on both."

Lavalle nods. "Absolutely."

"You arrested Mr. Birch just two days after Mr. Zimmer was killed."

"That's correct."

"Isn't that unusually fast?" Godfrey's obvious goal is to

insulate Lavalle from my trying to claim a rush to judgment. It's a good strategy.

"Yes, it is. But we make arrests when we think we have a provable case. We don't worry about the timing. If it takes three months, or if it takes a day, it doesn't matter. We follow the facts."

Godfrey nods. "Let's talk about those facts. What specifically made you certain that Mr. Birch was the guilty party?"

Lavalle is not going to get pinned down, even by a friendly question. "It was a combination of things. In terms of the Zimmer homicide, we had placed Mr. Birch near the scene, at the bar looking for Zimmer. We also had motive, and then when he was in possession of the murder weapon, there was no reason to wait any longer."

"What about the murder of Mr. Hackett?"

"Well, that was a different situation. Even though the actual homicide took place before that of Mr. Zimmer, it wasn't discovered until later. Mr. Birch was already in custody at that point. Once again there was motive, there was the same MO, and the dominant fact was that the gun used was the same. And it was found on Mr. Birch's property."

I'm surprised when Godfrey finishes his direct examination just before the lunch break. I thought he would drag it out much longer, even though Lavalle was technically not providing new information. I suspect that he wanted the jury to have the testimony to think about during lunch, so that it would set in before I tried to challenge it. It's an excellent strategy.

"Lieutenant Lavalle, I'd like to start with the shooting

of Mr. Hackett, since that happened before the Zimmer shooting," I say, once the lunch break is over. "I'd like you to imagine a situation in which you, or the Newark police, had discovered Mr. Hackett's body before Mr. Zimmer was shot."

He nods. "Very well."

"Thank you. Would you agree that in that hypothetical, you would not have had Mr. Birch's proximity to the murder scene, you would not have yet found the gun, and you would not have been aware of motive, since Mr. Birch had never threatened Mr. Hackett, in open court or otherwise."

Lavalle nods. "That's true."

"So you would not have made an arrest at that point, correct?"

"Not unless other facts were discovered."

"Now in this hypothetical, you are assigned to the Zimmer murder, which took place days after Mr. Hackett's body was found. Suddenly you have all this evidence: you have Mr. Birch near the scene, you have him having threatened Mr. Zimmer, and then you have the final piece that closes the deal, the gun and handkerchief on Mr. Birch's property. The arrest becomes an easy call, correct?"

"I was confident in the case, if that's what you mean. Yes."

"So once Mr. Zimmer was killed, everything fell into place?"

"We followed the evidence like we do in every case."

"But in your view Mr. Birch made it easy for you on the Zimmer shooting, did he not? He was at the scene, he spoke to the bartender. Then he killed someone that he had threatened in open court, after which he buried the gun and handkerchief on his own property. Isn't that making it easy for you?"

"Fortunately, people who commit crimes sometimes make errors, and we try to capitalize on them."

"Mr. Birch made a lot of obvious errors, wouldn't you say?"

"I would agree with that," Lavalle says, surprising me.

"Good. Let's talk about some of those errors. Mr. Birch showed up at the bar looking for Mr. Zimmer by name, is that correct?"

"Yes.

"He said that he was expecting to meet Mr. Zimmer there. Did you ever determine why he had that expectation?"

"We were unable to."

"Just in case the bartender could not identify him, Mr. Birch used his own credit card to pay his tab. Does that sound like someone who was about to commit a murder?"

"It was ill-advised at best."

"So Mr. Birch shoots Mr. Zimmer and then goes home after doing so. How far would you estimate it is from the shooting scene to Mr. Birch's house?"

"I wouldn't know."

"I drove it the other day and it measured sixteen miles. Does that seem about right?"

"I wouldn't argue the point."

"So Mr. Birch had sixteen miles during which he could have wiped his prints off the gun and dropped it anywhere, absolutely anywhere, and it could never have been tied to him. Is that correct?"

"It would certainly have been more difficult; I would never say never."

"But instead of doing that, he buried the gun on his own property, throwing a handkerchief in to close the deal. Did you find prints on the gun? There was not testimony to that effect."

"No, it was wiped clean."

"So your assumption is he wiped it clean and then buried it on his own property, thinking that the lack of prints would get him off the hook if it was found?"

"I don't know what he was thinking."

"Now, let's talk about finding the gun." I introduce a photograph of the dirt, before the gun was dug up. "Did you dig up the entire yard, or just this place where the gun was found?"

"Just the one place."

"Because it was so obvious that there was recent activity there?"

"Yes."

"Another stupid move by Mr. Birch, wouldn't you say? First he declined to put it anywhere else, where it couldn't be traced back to him, and then he put it in a place so obvious you couldn't help but look."

"It was a mistake on his part, yes."

"Was there a post in the ground with a sign saying GUN BURIED HERE?"

Godfrey objects and the judge sustains it and reprimands me.

"In your theory of the case, why do you think he included the handkerchief when he buried the gun?"

"Possibly to protect the gun, in case he wanted to use it again."

"Is it a good idea to bury a gun in dirt if you want to keep using it?" I ask.

"As I said, the handkerchief could have been used to protect the gun."

I hold up the handkerchief, which had been introduced as evidence during the prosecution's case. It is small, maybe nine inches square, and thin. "This is what he was using to protect the gun? Do you think a towel might have worked better?"

"Probably."

Next I display the police photo of the gun and hand-kerchief in the ground. The handkerchief is just loosely covering the gun and not protecting it at all. Then I show the police photo of the gun after the handkerchief was removed; the gun has dirt all over it. "This gun wasn't well protected by the handkerchief, was it, Lieutenant?"

"No, it was not."

"So the only forensics that tied the gun to Mr. Birch was the DNA on the handkerchief?"

"Correct. But it all was found in his yard."

"Yes. We're all aware of that. I noticed that in the prosecution's case there was no photograph of the shovel. Did you examine the shovel Mr. Birch used to dig the hole?"

"We did not find a shovel."

"Did you find any tool that had dirt on it, that he might have used? That might have had fingerprints on it?"

"We did not."

I feign surprise. "Really? Is it your theory of the case that Mr. Birch drove sixteen miles to place the murder weapon at his own home, but then took the time and effort to dispose of the shovel elsewhere?"

"I can't speak to that. We did not find a digging tool."

"But that didn't bother you; you were too busy following all this evidence that Mr. Birch provided." I smile. "Maybe you should have kept digging."

Godfrey objects and Judge Baron sustains. He tells Lavalle that he doesn't have to answer the question, even though I didn't ask a question.

"Lieutenant, did it trouble you at all when all this evidence was so easy to come by? Did it cause you any concern that maybe someone orchestrated it to make Mr. Birch appear guilty?"

"No, it did not."

"You just followed the road map that was left for you."

"We followed the evidence."

I nod and shake my head as if saddened by his answer. "Just like you were programmed to. No further questions."

Godfrey tries to rehabilitate Lavalle on his redirect examination. He's not particularly successful, but I honestly do not think it matters. All I was able to get across is that Tony would have to have been really stupid to leave the clues he left. The jury might have no problem thinking that a man on trial for a double murder is, in fact, really stupid.

When he's finished, Godfrey says, "Your Honor, the prosecution rests."

That means one thing.

It's our turn.

We are going to have to tackle this head-on," I say. Eddie Dowd and I are in my office, going over what can loosely be called the defense case.

He nods. "No fooling around; throw fastballs right down the middle and dare them to hit them."

I've decided that I can't hide Tony's past; it's the only way to bring Luther and the Blood Dragons into the case. Which is crucial because Luther and the Blood Dragons are our entire case. It will no doubt piss him off, but I suspect our home invasion the other night has already accomplished that.

To make matters worse, one of our main witnesses is going to be Chuck Holmes, Eddie's employee at his auto repair shop. He'll generally reference Tony's character, but, most important, he'll implicate Russell Estrada in the arson. Through other means, we'll tie Estrada to Luther.

"I need you to prep Chuck Holmes," I say. "It's not going to be easy. He'll be nervous and is not sharp in the moment. Everything direct and to the point; we don't want to leave openings for Godfrey on cross."

Eddie and I go over the approach and exactly where I

want to lead Chuck. I spoke to Chuck a little while ago when he picked up his check and discussed his testifying. I could see he was anxious about it, but when I told him it would help "Mr. Tony," he agreed.

Eddie is going to miss court tomorrow in order to prep Chuck, whose testimony will be the next day. I wish I could miss court tomorrow.

I head home, but first I stop at Willie's house. I haven't seen Zoey in a while, and Tony has asked about her a couple of times. Willie's not home, but Sondra is.

"Where's Willie?" I ask.

"I . . . I don't know."

With those words, Sondra conclusively demonstrates that she is the worst actress in America. She is nervous about something, something that obviously involves Willie's current location.

"What aren't you telling me?"

"Nothing . . . really."

Suddenly it hits me. "Is he following me?"

"Andy, Laurie will kill me."

"Call him. Never mind; I'll call him." I dial Willie's cell number and he answers with "Hey, Andy. What's going on? I'm at the market."

"No, you're not, you're outside watching me. So why not just come in?"

There's a hesitation. Then, "Okay."

He's here within a minute. Sondra says, "I'm sorry," then heads off to get Zoey.

"She told you?" Willie says.

"No, I figured it out. How long has Laurie had you doing this?"

He shrugs. "A couple of days; I cover when Marcus can't."

Laurie tends to secretly have me followed and protected when she thinks I might be in danger . . . when I've pissed off the wrong people. Luther certainly qualifies as one of those people. Sometimes she tells me, sometimes she doesn't, but nothing I say can deter her.

"You can stop now. I can take care of myself."

He smiles. "Yeah." Then, "I take my orders from Laurie."

I return the smile. "So do I."

Sondra comes in with Zoey, who comes over to me to receive the requisite petting. "How is she doing?" I ask.

Sondra shrugs. "Okay. I wouldn't describe her as happy, but she's doing all right. At least she hasn't tried to run away again."

"You gonna win the case?" Willie has a way of coming to the point.

"I'm trying, Willie. I'm trying." Then, "I haven't seen you in court lately."

"I know. It makes me too nervous. I don't know how you do it."

I nod. "Maybe I should retire."

We open our case by calling Ben Rutland.

He has nothing to do with the case itself, but will instead function as one of our character witnesses.

We're going to need this character testimony as a "buffer" before we get to the serious stuff, meaning Tony's life in the gang and his less-than-legitimate past exploits. When the jury hears the bad news, I want them to be aware he has since turned his life around.

Rutland is in his late sixties, a gruff, grizzled type who gives off the vibe that he does not suffer fools gladly or at all. He is wearing a suit and tie, and I would guess he has previously done so only at weddings and funerals.

"Mr. Rutland, what is your occupation?"

"I'm a retired auto mechanic."

"How long have you been retired?"

"Close to a year and a half."

"Can you describe your connection to Mr. Birch?"

"He came to work for me in my shop and then bought it from me a couple of years later when I retired."

"When you hired him, had you been aware that he had once served time in prison for involuntary manslaughter?"

I'm going to get the bad news out of the way before God-frey can do it.

"Yes. He got into a fight and punched a guy. I'd hate to tell you how many times I've done that."

I pause to try and not smile at the answer. "Was Mr. Birch a good and reliable employee?"

"Best I ever had."

"You had no concerns about his handling your money, or dealing with your customers?"

"If I did, I wouldn't have sold him my shop. I loved that place, and he built it into a better business than when I owned it. And now the bastards burned it down."

Godfrey objects and asks for a bench conference, during which he complains that what Rutland just blurted out is prejudicial and irrelevant, though I have no idea how it could be both. I explain that I won't pursue it with this witness, though I will bring it out later in the defense case, and it will be very relevant.

I just have a few more questions for Rutland, mostly to demonstrate his respect and warm feelings for Tony, and then I turn him over to Godfrey.

He treats Rutland as if he is of no importance, which might well be true. "Mr. Rutland, how long has it been since you've had contact with Mr. Birch?"

"Maybe six months; I stopped in to see how he was doing."

"Do you have any personal knowledge as to whether or not Mr. Birch committed these crimes?"

"He wouldn't."

"Please answer the question I asked. Do you have any personal knowledge as to whether or not Mr. Birch com-mitted these crimes?"

"No."

"Thank you."

I am sure Godfrey is delighted to get Rutland off the stand. I don't think Godfrey is going to like the next one either. Her name is Kathryn Spivey, and she was reluctant to testify, agreeing to do so only after Tony signed a release.

I take Ms. Spivey through her impressive academic credentials and establish that she was Tony's psychotherapist for eighteen months, which ended about six months ago.

"You take contemporaneous notes during your sessions?" I ask.

"Yes. Always."

"And have you reviewed those notes in preparation for your testimony today?"

"Yes."

In less colorful terms that Rutland, Spivey reports that Tony came to her to allow him to understand and come to terms with the gang life he had led. He was intent on turning that around, and she has no doubt that he had successfully done so. "In fact," she says, "that is why we stopped our sessions. He had accomplished his goals."

Godfrey treats Spivey as insignificant, as he did with Rutland, though this time he gets better results. She is cautious in her responses and certainly admits that she has no knowledge of Tony's activities in the past six months, including whether he actually committed these crimes.

It's been a decent morning. Nothing has been accomplished that will win the case, but a base has been established. Time for lunch.

As soon as I get out into the hall, I call Eddie Dowd.

"How is it going with Chuck?"

"Pretty well, I think. Not a home run, but a double in the gap. We spent three hours this morning, and he's coming back after lunch."

"You think he can be effective?"

"I think so. But he's nervous. He's anxious talking in front of me; in that courtroom he's going to struggle to keep it under control. But bottom line, I'd keep him in the lineup. He loves Tony and is desperate to do anything he can to help."

"Okay. Keep working with him."

"Will do."

I have some trepidation about calling Chuck, but his testimony is essential. I just have to count on Eddie to get him through it.

My first witness this afternoon is Sergeant Chris Carbajal of the New Jersey State Police. For the past fifteen years he has been dealing with street gangs, acting as a liaison to local law enforcement.

After I establish that, I ask him if he had been familiar

with Tony through his work. "Yes, I heard the name and knew about him. He was part of a small group called the Fulton Street Boyz."

"How many members did they have?"

"Not many . . . maybe ten. It would fluctuate a bit."

"Was there a hierarchy that you know of?"

"Yes, there were essentially four people in the top rung. Mr. Birch, Mr. Zimmer, Mr. Hackett, and TJ Richardson."

"Where is TJ Richardson today?"

"He was murdered in prison."

"Why was he in prison?"

"He was involved in a gun battle during an alleged mugging. The intended victim pulled out a gun, and Richardson returned the fire. A stray bullet hit and killed an eight-year-old girl. Her name was Julie Sanford."

"Why do you say an *alleged* mugging?" I ask.

"Because that was the way it was portrayed. In actuality Richardson was collecting a debt in a drug deal."

"Who was he collecting it from?"

"A man named Josh Winkler."

"Where is Mr. Winkler today?"

"He was murdered last week."

Godfrey jumps up. "Objection, Your Honor. I'm sure we all find this fascinating, but it bears no relevance to our case."

"Your Honor, perhaps Mr. Godfrey was out sick the day they covered relevant testimony in law school. I could recommend an excellent correspondence course."

"Gentlemen, gentlemen . . . objection overruled. Mr. Carpenter, I will give you some latitude, but that has its limits. As does my tolerance for your sarcasm."

"Yes, Your Honor. . . . Sergeant Carbajal, just to be clear, Mr. Winkler was murdered while Mr. Birch was in custody and on trial?"

"Yes."

"Back to the gangs. Was there a hierarchy involved? Did the Fulton Street gang take orders from anyone else?"

"Oh, yes. There is a gang called the Blood Dragons, which controls gang activity in this area and beyond. They would give out assignments, collections or whatever, to their satellite operations and give them a cut of the profits. It's big business."

"Is there a leader of the Blood Dragons?"

"Yes. His name is Luther, but he would have people to deal with the lesser gangs."

"Do you know which of his people dealt with the group Mr. Birch was affiliated with?"

"I believe it was a man named Russell Estrada."

I introduce as a defense exhibit the photograph of Estrada taken by the security camera at the auto repair shop. "Is this Mr. Estrada?"

"It is."

"And where is Mr. Estrada today?"

"Dead. He was killed two days ago."

"While Mr. Birch was in custody and on trial?"

"Yes."

I turn the witness over to Godfrey, who frowns as if frustrated he has to deal with this nonsense.

"Sergeant, do you have any independent knowledge at all as to who murdered Franklin Zimmer and Raymond Hackett?"

"I do not."

"It is not a case you have worked on?"

"It is not."

"Was Mr. Birch in custody and on trial when they were killed?"

"He was not."

"Thank you."

It would be hard for Luther to remember the last time he was worried.

There were always minor annoyances—fires to extinguish, discipline to be dealt out—but nothing that represented a significant threat to his authority. And his personal safety was always assured; until recently he would have put his security on a par with the US president's.

But that had changed, a reality that was dramatically brought home by the invasion of his home last week. That followed the incident in the park with Russell Estrada, which one of the bodyguards had foolishly spoken about. Then came the murder of Estrada and the two bodyguards.

Luther was sure that the other members of the Blood Dragons thought that Luther had ordered the deaths of Estrada and the others as punishment for the park incident, but he had not. He might have considered it, but they were gunned down before he had decided whether to take any action.

He couldn't be positive where all the threats were coming from. Obviously a prime candidate would be the lawyer and the others who invaded his home. They might have killed Estrada, but somehow Luther didn't think so. If they were inclined in that direction, they could easily have killed Estrada that night in the park.

More likely the threat was coming from a rival, or at least an aspiring one. It could have been a gang member chafing to take power, whether from outside the Blood Dragons or from within. Luther had a good intelligence operation that usually tipped him off to things like this, but this time it had let him down.

All of that is why Luther called a meeting of what could loosely be called his "council." It consisted of himself and his three "lieutenants." Russell Estrada would have been part of this group meeting; instead his murder was one of the reasons it was taking place.

The meeting was in Passaic, in one of the offices behind Chasers Pub, a downtown bar that Luther owned, though his name would not be found on the ownership papers. This was the office that Luther most often worked out of, though he used two others as well. Outside the office were six of Luther's "soldiers"; this was not a meeting that anyone was going to interrupt.

The bar itself was operating as usual, with patrons having no idea that such a momentous meeting was taking place nearby. It was late, ten o'clock on a weekday winter evening, so the place was not at all crowded. To be exact, five people were there, including the bartender.

One of the patrons sat near the middle of the bar, typing into his phone. Another, with two shopping bags from local Passaic stores, sat at the far right of the bar, nursing his second beer. A couple in their thirties sat near the front window, but they were already signaling to settle their tab.

Luther, as was his style, let the others in the back office offer their views on what was happening and what had to be done about it. His management style was not to give any indication which way he was leaning, since he knew that would inhibit the others. Once he set the tone, they would play to him, which might stifle any good ideas they might have.

No one had any indication that there were rivals out there. They all felt that their intelligence tentacles would have tipped them off, but everything had been completely quiet in that regard.

What none of them would say openly, knowing it would be a fatal mistake, was that down deep they all believed Luther had Estrada and the two bodyguards killed. It was the only thing that made sense.

But basically the three reached a consensus, summed up by the man they called Paco: "The lawyer has to die. People like that can't come into your home the way they did. If he lives, the word will get around and might give people ideas. If he dies, the word will get around the way we want it to."

Luther nodded, pleased that his lieutenants had come to the same decision he had already made. The lawyer had to die, and if any of the others that were with him happened to get in the way, they would meet the same fate.

The group spent the next forty minutes planning the operation. Luther would commission two people to find out where the lawyer lived. That would be no problem;

they could just follow him home from the courtroom. Then, once they understood his patterns and habits, they could decide how best to kill him.

They finished the meeting at eleven. The bar was almost closed. The couple near the window were gone, as was the man who had come in with the shopping bags. He had stupidly forgotten one that contained a large toy, probably for his kid, because he was so drunk that he could barely stagger out of the bar.

The only people left were the bartender and the guy with the phone.

The explosion killed both of them, along with Luther and his entire "council."

The whole building was obliterated, and the two buildings on either side sustained substantial damage.

It would be fair to say that vacancies had been created in the Blood Dragons' chain of command.

'm much more anxious than usual about tomorrow's court session.

Chuck Holmes could easily crumble under the pressure of testifying; this is a guy who is not accustomed to public speaking. Nor is he someone likely to think quickly on his feet, which Godfrey can take enormous advantage of.

Part of my anxiety stems from my not being able to prep him. That job went to Eddie Dowd simply because I was in court all day. He is optimistic that Chuck will come through, and I have come to trust Eddie, but I'd still feel better if I had been more hands on.

I've even considered having Eddie conduct the direct examination of Chuck, but I'm afraid that will be a red flag to alert the jury and Godfrey that something is wrong. I'm just going to try to get Chuck to tell his story and get him off the stand.

Tonight, after walking Tara and Sebastian, I've been going over the discovery and trial documents for what seems like the ten millionth time. I'm not learning anything new; there is nothing new to learn.

The most interesting part of the night is that Laurie

has twice come by to ask if I'm going to be up late. That's usually a sign that she might be interested in some bedroom activity, and I have a simple rule about that. When it's not during a trial, if she's interested, I'm interested. If it's during a trial . . . if she's interested, I'm interested.

It's eleven fifteen, and I can't look at these documents anymore. I've also gone over more than I need to how I'm going to handle our witnesses; I like to maintain some spontaneity.

"Andy, come on up here." It's Laurie's voice, calling from the bedroom. It is not a request I am going to refuse.

I take the stairs two steps at a time, so I'm in the bedroom within thirty seconds of her calling me. Based on past experience, I don't think that's enough time for her to get out of the mood.

One look at her tells me that she's not in the mood at all. She's sitting at the end of the bed, staring intently at the television. It's the local NBC affiliate, covering what looks to be a large fire.

The next thing I notice is that at the bottom of the screen it says, "Explosion in Passaic bar."

"What the hell is that?"

"A building blew up in downtown Passaic. They said that twelve people are dead, mostly gang members."

Somehow I instinctively believe I know who it is: "Luther."

Laurie picks up the phone and calls Corey. Based on her side of the conversation, it appears that he's been watching the news as well.

Their conversation is brief, and when she gets off, she

says, "He has some contacts at Passaic PD; he's going to make some calls and see what he can find out."

My evening has taken a decidedly unwelcome turn, and I don't mean because Luther may have bitten the dust. It's forty-five minutes before Corey calls back, and Laurie tells him that she's putting him on the speakerphone so that I can hear.

"Luther is one of the dead," he says. "Along with some of his top people and some bodyguards. There also were two fatalities in the bar itself. It's such a mess that they're not sure of the total, but it looks like at least eleven dead."

"How was it done?" Laurie asks.

"They're not there yet, but it appears that the explosion source was in the bar."

This changes things for me. "Corey, I'm going to need to subpoena somebody from Passaic PD to testify about this. Very straightforward . . . just the facts."

"I'll try and get you a name." He also promises to keep digging for information, though he's not likely to learn much more until morning. By then the media will probably have dug out the story as well.

I have absolutely no idea what this means for our case, if anything. But I'm going to have to figure it out by tomorrow.

s it true?" Tony asks, when he's brought into court. "Is Luther really dead?"

"Certainly seems to be," I say. "Any idea who might have done it?"

He doesn't hesitate. "It's got to be someone that was under him. Someone who wants to take over. Either that or it's part of a gang war; some other gang decided they didn't want to continue taking orders. They want to give them."

"How does a gang like the Blood Dragons pick a new leader?"

He shrugs. "Beats the hell out of me."

I wish this was a weekend, so that court would not be in session. But it's not, and Judge Baron comes in and slams down his gavel like he does every day. Time to go back to work.

Eddie Dowd is once again not at the defense table. He is outside, having coffee with Chuck Holmes. His goal is to keep Chuck calm, to assure him that the actual testimony will be quick and painless. He's not going over the details anymore; he's already confident that Chuck knows the drill, and Eddie doesn't want to overdo it.

Chuck will be our second witness today. Our first is Lieutenant Ernie Brewster, who is in charge of the gang unit in the Paterson PD. He is the successor to George Koontz, who I spoke to in Pete Stanton's office.

"Lieutenant Brewster, did I ask you to review the testimony earlier in this trial of Lieutenant Carbajal of the New Jersey State Police?"

"You did, and I did review it."

"He testified that Russell Estrada was a key lieutenant in the Blood Dragons gang, reporting to the leader, a man named Luther. You reviewed that part?"

"I did."

"You are in charge of the unit in the Paterson Police Department that deals with gangs and gang violence?"

"Yes, sir."

"Was Lieutenant Carbajal correct in his assessment of Mr. Estrada's position within the Blood Dragons gang?"

"He was."

Brewster is a man of few words; I like that. "Lieutenant Carbajal also said that Mr. Estrada was recently murdered. Are you familiar with the circumstances of that murder?"

"Yes, it's my case to work on."

"Please describe what happened."

"Estrada and two of his bodyguards were out doing their rounds, meaning they were making collections and making sure their operations were running smoothly. They made a stop on Market Street in Paterson, and as they were leaving, the three men were gunned down by semiautomatic fire. The perpetrator escaped undetected."

"Do you have any suspects?"

"The investigation is ongoing."

I'm not going to introduce the events of last night; I'll do that later. My hope and expectation is that the jury knows about it anyway through news reports. "Thank you. No further questions."

Godfrey by now has a permanent frown on his face. It's as if he wants to apologize to the jury for putting them through this obvious waste of time. He stands up to cross-examine Brewster.

"Lieutenant, to your knowledge, does the murder of Mr. Estrada and the two others have anything to do with the murders of Mr. Zimmer and Hackett?"

"I'm not aware of a connection."

"Thank you."

Judge Baron takes a ten-minute break, which is well timed for me, because Corey has just walked into the courtroom with a man that I don't recognize. I head back to him, and he introduces Sergeant Daniel Moore of the Passaic Police Department.

"Thanks for coming," I say, after Corey introduces us.

"It wasn't my idea. I was threatened with a subpoena."

"Sorry. I promise this will be painless. You'll be on and off in no time."

When court is back in session, I call Sergeant Moore.

Godfrey objects, claiming correctly that Moore was not on our witness list.

"Your Honor, events from last night which we could not have anticipated prompted our calling Sergeant Moore. I have not even had a chance to talk to him myself."

Judge Baron says, "I will let the witness testify.

Mr. Godfrey, if you'd like, I will grant you a short continuance to prepare, or you can have one after the direct examination of Sergeant Moore."

"Thank you, Your Honor. With your permission, I will delay that option until we hear what the witness has to say."

The judge is fine with that, as am I. And then I hope Godfrey demands and gets a four-month continuance.

"Sergeant Moore, there has been testimony in this case about a man named Russell Estrada. Are you familiar with him?"

"I am."

"There was also testimony that he was murdered the other night along with two of his colleagues. Are you aware of that as well?"

Moore nods. "Yes."

"Is it a case you are working on?"

"No. That murder happened in Paterson, so it is being handled by Paterson PD. I am handling a related case."

"Which one would that be?"

"Last night there was an explosion at a bar in Passaic. Eleven people were killed, nine of whom were members of the Blood Dragons."

"Is that the same gang that Estrada and the two other men who were killed with him belonged to?"

"It is."

I shake my head as if in wonderment. "They're dropping like flies."

Godfrey starts to stand to object, but then stops. I have a hunch he can't think of a legal reason to object; "Carpenter is obnoxious" doesn't qualify.

Moore treats it as a serious question. "There have been a lot of deaths in the gang world lately, yes."

"Sergeant, included in the earlier testimony was a reference to the late Mr. Estrada's boss, the leader of the Blood Dragons. His name is Luther. Can you tell us his current status?"

"He died along with his three top lieutenants in the explosion last night."

I turn Moore over to Godfrey, who treats him in the same manner he treated the previous witness. He just gets him to confirm that he is unaware of any connection whatsoever between the explosion and the murders of Zimmer and Hackett.

We adjourn for lunch.

Next up is Chuck Holmes.

'***'ve taken a big chance by saving Chuck Holmes for last.

The reason I am doing it is that he most clearly connects the Blood Dragons and their attitude toward Tony. But I recognize the danger that Chuck will crack under cross-examination. Either way it will be the last testimony the jury hears, which elevates its importance significantly.

I meet up with Chuck and Eddie briefly in the cafeteria during lunch. I don't talk about his testimony; I just smile and tell him that everything will be fine, and that "Mr. Tony" appreciates his help.

He seems nervous but under control, and he smiles at the mention of Tony. I think he'll be okay; the advantage we have is that he is telling the complete truth, so there shouldn't be much opportunity for Godfrey to trip him up.

Court resumes, and I call Chuck to the stand. Here goes . . .

"Mr. Holmes, what is your occupation?"

"I am a mechanic. I work on cars."

I can hear the nervousness in his voice. That could

cut in our favor; the jury could be sympathetic to him. "Where do you work?"

"It's called TB Auto Repair."

"Does *TB* stand for 'Tony Birch'?"

"Yes, sir."

"So you work for Mr. Birch?"

"Yes, sir."

"Do you like your job?"

He brightens noticeably. "Yes, sir. I like it a lot."

"And Mr. Birch . . . do you like working for him?"

His voice gets louder and more confident. "Yes, sir."

"How long has it been since you've actually done some work there?"

"Well, there wasn't much to do when Mr. Tony was arrested. And then the fire . . ."

"There was a fire at the auto shop?"

"Yes, sir."

The jury has already heard about the fire, so I don't push it. I show Chuck the photograph of Estrada that was taken by the security camera at the auto repair shop. It was previously identified as him by Sergeant Carbajal of the State Police.

"Do you know where this photograph was taken?"

Chuck nods. "Yes, sir. It was at the shop. We have a camera that takes pictures of people."

"What happened when he came in that day?"

Chuck hesitates, as if he's trying to remember what he is supposed to say. "Well, I wasn't there; I was having some lunch. Sometimes I bring my own lunch, and sometimes I go out."

He seems to be losing focus; I've got to bring him back. "When you came back, was he there?"

Chuck nods. "Yes, sir. He was in Mr. Tony's office, looking through his desk."

"What did you do?"

"I said he couldn't do that. He wasn't allowed back there."

"What did he do?"

"He said a bad word and then he left. He was very angry; I thought he was going to hurt me."

"Were you afraid?"

Chuck seems embarrassed when he says, "A little bit. He was very mad."

"How long after that did the fire happen?"

"The next day."

"Was it a bad fire?"

"Yes, sir."

"So you can't work there anymore?"

Chuck almost looks like he's going to cry; I selfishly wish he would. But he holds it together. "I can't."

I turn him over to Godfrey for cross-examination. He has two options; he can go hard at Chuck and try to trip him up, or he can pretend to be sympathetic and go easy on him. I have no doubt that his decision will depend on his view of how the jury is reacting to Chuck.

"Mr. Holmes, on a normal workday, do you leave at the same time as Mr. Birch?"

"Mr. Tony hasn't been there; he has been here."

"I understand. I meant in the past, when he had been there. Did you leave work at the same time?"

"Sometimes. Sometimes he stayed later."

"Did you see him after you left? Did you often have dinner together or go to his house?"

Chuck shakes his head no, and Judge Baron tells him he has to speak, not just shake his head. So he does.

"So you did not spend a lot of time with Mr. Birch outside of work?"

"Once we had lunch at the diner."

Godfrey smiles a condescending smile. "So you didn't know what he did at night, or where he went?"

"No, sir."

Godfrey holds up the picture of Estrada. "Do you know why this man was in Mr. Birch's office?"

"He was looking for something."

"Do you know what he was looking for?"

"No."

"Did you ever see him again?"

"No."

"Never saw his picture on television, or in the news-paper?"

"No; I don't have a television. I don't read . . . any newspaper."

"Do you know who set the fire?"

"Yes," Chuck says, and I sense an impending disaster.

Godfrey feigns surprise. "Really? Who set the fire?"

"The man in that picture."

"How do you know that?" Godfrey asks, leading Chuck and me to the edge of a legal cliff.

Chuck has a deer-in-the-headlights look. He's afraid he's said the wrong thing, and he can't think of a way out. "I just know," he says.

"Who told you?" Godfrey asks, his voice insistent.

"Mr. Carpenter," Chuck says, then looks at me help-lessly.

"Isn't that interesting. . . . What else did Mr. Carpenter coach you to say?"

"I . . . I don't know."

"Thank you, Mr. Holmes. No further questions."

Judge Baron tells Chuck he is finished and can step down. He walks toward the gallery, as does Eddie Dowd. I pat Chuck on the shoulder as he goes by.

He did the best he could, but the bottom line is he hurt our case by making our tactics seem sketchy.

I should not have put him on the stand.

You can call off Willie and Marcus," I say when I get home. I hadn't said anything about it to Laurie before, but I just can't resist.

"You knew about that?"

"I am Andy Carpenter; I see all and know all."

She shrugs, unimpressed. "Good for you." Then, "I already called them off. Once Luther left the playing field, I couldn't think of anyone to protect you from."

"You've seen me in action, so you should know I don't need protection."

"Yeah, you're a tough guy."

"Yet I also have my sensitive side."

She doesn't consider that worthy of a response and instead asks me how Chuck did on the stand.

"Better than I expected. I was proud of him."

"So what are your chances?"

Laurie knows that I hate that question; it forces me to confront reality. I'm much more comfortable in the land of denial. "Slim. The best we can hope for is a couple of jurors to hang it. But that is just delaying the inevitable."

"Let me ask you this. Who do you think killed Estrada?"

"I thought it was Luther, as retribution for the night in Eastside Park. But now I don't know. It's possible it was the first shot in a gang war, and the explosion at the bar was the main event."

"So someone looking to take over the Blood Dragons?"

I nod. "That has to be it. Once it shakes out and somebody assumes control, we'll have our suspect. But even though I will tell the jury otherwise, I don't see how it relates to our case."

"Why not?"

"Because why would they start a gang war by killing Zimmer and Hackett and framing Tony? It doesn't fit."

She nods her agreement. Then, "Closing statements tomorrow?"

"Yes. One of the jurors has a doctor's appointment in the afternoon, so Judge Baron is going to wait until Monday to give the charge. But we're going to get the statements done tomorrow."

"So you are going to be working late on it tonight?"

"Not really; I'm set." I don't like to overprepare for opening and closing statements. I know the points I want to get across, and I find I can do so more effectively when I do it more spontaneously.

"Good. Because I was looking forward to spending some time in bed with you last night. Then the explosion killed all those people."

"I hate when that happens."

"Maybe we can make up for it tonight," she says.

"Let's not turn on the television. Just in case."

She smiles. "Good idea. We can listen to music."

"Great. Can it not involve reindeers?"

know you've heard a lot of talking in this courtroom," Godfrey says with an irritating smile.

"You've probably had more than enough. I know I've done a lot of it, and I'm sorry for that, but it couldn't be helped. I started it off with my opening statement, and I'd like you to think back to that for a moment.

"I told you how important your task was, how it is the foundation on which our justice system is built. But I also told you that as important as your job was, it was also going to be relatively easy. I told you that we were going to prove our case beyond a reasonable doubt, and I believe we have done just that.

"When you clear away all the smoke and all the distractions, the facts are as clear as can be. I know you've heard them all, but let me sum them up for you.

"Frankie Zimmer and Raymond Hackett were both gunned down, shot from behind, one bullet in the back of the head. But that's not the only thing they had in common. They were also in the same street gang as Mr. Birch; in fact, they were in the leadership group of four with him.

"And that's not all. They also both testified against the defendant when he was convicted of involuntary manslaughter. He considered that a betrayal. How do we know that? He threatened Mr. Zimmer's life in open court, in front of the judge, jury, court clerk, bailiffs, lawyers, and gallery.

"How much of a temper, a seething anger, does one have to have to do something like that? When Mr. Carpenter tells you that his client would never behave so self-destructively, I would point you to that incident. He could not control himself then, and he could not control himself now. It was not a mistake, as Mr. Carpenter would have you believe. It was an explosion of rage.

"But just threatening to kill someone who is then murdered does not prove guilt. If that is all the evidence we had, none of us would be here today. So let's examine the other evidence.

"Mr. Birch, after years of no contact with Mr. Zimmer, suddenly showed up at a bar that he frequented, looking for him. He said that he was supposed to meet him there, a claim that Mr. Zimmer subsequently denied to the bartender. And why did he make that claim? What made him believe there was a meeting to be held? Well, we don't know. We never heard any testimony about that."

Something that Godfrey just said jogs something in my mind. Mind-jogging bothers me when I can't get in touch with the cause. At this moment I can't, but I will try to connect with it later.

Godfrey continues, "So Mr. Birch left the bar and laid in wait for Mr. Zimmer to walk home, a walk he made very often. But Mr. Zimmer never made it home; the defendant saw to that.

"But even with all that, he could possibly have gotten away with it, had we not found the murder weapon. It was buried on his property, along with a handkerchief to protect it, possibly so he could dig it up and use it again. And that handkerchief had his DNA on it.

"Mr. Carpenter claims that this is all one massive frame-up. But who did the framing? And why did they do it? And while we're at it, how did the real murderer wind up with the defendant's handkerchief? We haven't heard a word about any of that."

Something else just jogged my mind. I can't place it yet, but my mind is starting to get clogged with jogs. It's frustrating, but I've learned that the best way to connect with it is to not try.

"I will admit that the defendant made errors in trying to cover his tracks," Godfrey says. "I'm grateful for that; we should all be grateful for that. His quick arrest might well have prevented more killings. He's not a master criminal, but he is a deadly and violent one.

"You may not be surprised to hear this, but our jails are not filled with Rhodes scholars. Every single one of the prisoners there made a mistake that enabled their capture. Mr. Birch will fit right in.

"You came here to serve honorably and do your duty. This is your time. Thank you."

Much as I hate to admit it, Godfrey did an excellent job.

My turn.

Mr. Birch is not proud of everything he's done in his life," I say.

"We've been very up-front about that. He grew up on the streets . . . tough, difficult streets, and he did some wrong things in an effort to get by.

"But I'll tell you what he is proud of, and that is turning his life around. You've heard testimony to that effect. He taught himself to be a mechanic, then he worked as a loyal employee, and then he managed to buy the business when the owner retired. The former owner told you that he trusted Mr. Birch with his money and ultimately with the business he loved.

"Mr. Godfrey told you that when Mr. Birch accused Mr. Zimmer of betrayal in that courtroom, he demonstrated an uncontrollable temper. Well, I wish all people with uncontrollable tempers could control them that well.

"He apparently controlled it for six years. Six years in which he could have planned these killings, six years to do it in a way that detection would have been difficult. Not necessarily impossible; law enforcement does a good job. But far more difficult.

"Take the killing of Mr. Hackett. There were no clues; the detective in charge of the case admitted that. It was a shooting at night, with no obvious evidence to connect it to anyone.

"Now look at the Zimmer killing. Couldn't that have been done the same way? Mr. Birch obviously knew that Mr. Zimmer frequented that bar; he didn't have to go in and pretend to have a meeting scheduled with him. He could have just laid in wait and fired the shot. Then he could have wiped the gun clean and disposed of it any-where.

"But that's not what Mr. Godfrey would have you believe that he did. No, in Mr. Godfrey's narrative, he buried the gun on his own property, throwing in a handkerchief with his DNA on it. You've seen the photograph of the overturned dirt; the only thing missing was a neon sign flashing LOOK HERE, OFFICERS."

"Please bear with me for a few moments; I want to read you some names. Franklin Zimmer, Raymond Hackett, Russell Estrada, Josh Winkler, Robert Simeone, Ronald Pisano, Carl Baker, Randall Lambert, Jose Angelos, John Sarnow, Louis Ornellos, Joaquin Carreon, George Spinney, Duane Weaver, Luther Roman."

I pause to let the list of names sink in. I hadn't even known Luther's last name; media reports referred to him only as Luther. It took Sam Willis to uncover it.

I continue, "You know about Mr. Zimmer and Mr. Hackett. Mr. Winkler was shot down in a rest area on the Palisades Interstate. Mr. Estrada, Mr. Simeone, and Mr. Pisano were gunned down on a Paterson street the other night. All of the others, including the leader, Luther Roman, were killed in the explosion at the bar in Passaic.

"All of them were directly involved with gangs, except for Mr. Winkler, who was a customer of theirs. But here's the important fact to understand: of those fifteen deaths, thirteen took place while Anthony Birch was in custody and on trial.

"There is a gang war going on. I don't know why; I don't even know all the players. But the Zimmer and Hackett killings were merely the first shots fired. It obviously exploded out of control, and it became much bigger and couldn't be contained. Once that happened, it grew to a point where efforts to blame Mr. Birch became untenable.

"Judge Baron will instruct you on how to proceed . . . how to deliberate. He will talk to you about reasonable doubt, and how if you have such doubt about Mr. Birch's guilt, you must vote to acquit.

"I would ask, how could you not? How can you be positive that the Zimmer and Hackett killings were separate and apart from all of the others? Isn't it at least possible? Isn't it reasonable to assume that they might all be connected?

"If the answer to those questions is yes, then it is your duty to vote to acquit Mr. Birch and end this nightmare. He is not a murderer; he is a man who wants to live in peace. It is up to you to grant him that.

"Thank you."

I go back to the defense table with the same sinking

feeling I have had after every single closing argument I have ever given. I have done everything I could, and it is out of my hands from here on in.

I hate the loss of control; it makes me physically ill.

Willie is sitting in the front row, and I want to tell him this is all his fault.

But I don't.

He's my friend.

This is an unusual, slightly disorienting situation for me.

I have a whole series of ridiculous superstitions that I observe during a wait for a verdict. I'm tempted to kick them into gear, but the problem is that, even though the work of the lawyers is over, the jury hasn't gotten the case yet.

If I start observing them now, the Superstition God might get pissed off and put a reverse hex on me. But if I don't start now, then it feels like there is absolutely nothing I can do to influence the situation.

I need a diversion, which is why I have come to Charlie's tonight. If I drink enough beer, eat enough french fries, and watch enough sports, there is a chance I won't obsess about the trial. A small chance.

Vince Sanders and Pete Stanton are already in place when I arrive, which is not exactly a news event. The televisions are all tuned to basketball, mostly NBA games, with a couple of college games thrown in. The college football season is over, and the NFL playoffs are well underway.

I haven't had the time to follow the playoffs closely because of the intensity of the trial. There is a chance my lack of focus will cause me to be drummed out of the Sports Degenerates Union.

"Lavalle said you never laid a glove on him on your cross-examination," Pete says. He's talking about Lieutenant James Lavalle, who is in charge of the Birch case under Pete.

I laugh. "I chewed him up and spit him out. Except for you, I've never had more fun destroying a cop on the stand." My cross on Lavalle was actually only fairly effective, but I'm obviously not going to tell Pete that.

He returns the laugh. "How long do you think it will take the jury to find Birch guilty? The over-under is an hour; I took the under."

"If you win, you can use the money to pay for your beer."

"Boys, boys . . . ," Vince says. Any hint of me not paying their tab at Charlie's is enough to scare Vince into a peacemaker role.

"Any chance you solved the Russell Estrada murder?" I ask.

"Not yet," Pete says.

"Any chance you've ever solved any murder? With you in charge of Homicide, every murder should immediately go into the cold-case file."

Vince, who has been covering the case for his newspaper, says, "Hey, give Pete a break. It's hard for him to keep up; dead bodies follow you wherever you go. Luther, Estrada, Winkler, all the other gang guys . . . you walk around with a dark cloud over your head."

"What did you say?" I ask, although I know exactly what Vince said.

He repeats it, but adds, "Having said that, I hope it doesn't cause you to reconsider paying the tab here."

"Vince, don't worry about it. What you just said has earned you free food and beer for the rest of your natural, albeit pathetic, life."

I turn to Pete and say, "You around this weekend?"

"I'll be right here. Where else am I going to be?"

"Good. I'll be in touch. Stay by the phone."

With that I get up and leave. As I do, I can hear Pete grunt, "Yeah, right."

I want to get home right away to talk this out with Laurie and see if she thinks I'm onto something. But in my gut I know I am.

Once I get in the car, I call Sam Willis. As always, he answers on the first ring; I think the phone must be stapled to his ear.

"Sam, I need you to try and find something for me. But you've got to be really careful; everything depends on it."

I tell him what it is, and he says, "I'm on it, Chief."

'm in the office at ten o'clock in the morning.

I can't remember the last time I've been in the office on a Saturday, possibly because I've never been in the office on a Saturday. But it's going to be my base of operations for the next part of my job.

The first call I make is to Sam, and I put him on the speakerphone. "Sam, there's a guy named Jesus Munoz. I believe he might live in Elizabeth. He's a gang leader; the gang is called the Ghetto Saints. I already know a lot about him; but I want to know even more. I have to be able to slam-dunk this guy."

"I'm on it."

"I also want any information you can get me on Eugene Sanford. He was the father of the little girl shot by TJ Richardson when he tried to collect from Josh Winkler."

"I'm on it."

"I need everything by tomorrow."

"No problem." Sam is aware that everything I have just said is total bull, but he handles it like a pro.

Eddie Dowd comes by at ten fifteen, as we have planned.

I've already spoken to Eddie, so he basically knows what's going on.

"I'm going to ask the judge to reopen testimony on Monday morning," I say.

"On what basis? Judges don't like to do that."

"I know, but I'm going to have compelling evidence."

"I'm all ears."

"Okay. For one thing, there's a guy named Jesus Munoz. He is the top guy in a street gang in Elizabeth that has not aligned with the Blood Dragons. I am in possession of evidence that not only implicates him in all these murders, but also proves that he had a grudge against Zimmer, Hackett, and Tony Birch, going back years."

"Wow."

"Wow is right. And there's more. I think I can show that Eugene Sanford, the father of the little girl shot to death, was actually involved in the drug trade with Luther. It was no coincidence that he was on the scene that day."

"How does that help our case?"

"It muddies the water even more. Just another element to make the jury find reasonable doubt."

"Where is this Sanford guy now?"

"He died about two years after the incident in a car crash. So he won't be here to defend himself, but I can live with that."

Eddie laughs. "When can I hear the details?"

"Meet me here Monday morning at seven o'clock. We can talk about how to present it to the judge."

"Will you have documents?"

"No, for the time being it will all be in my head. But

I can make it stick. With that and especially the Munoz evidence, I really think Tony will walk."

"Sounds great. Monday morning at seven."

We both leave, and I head home to spend what shows every sign of being the longest weekend of my life. I'll watch the NFL playoff games, but they won't supply the required diversion.

I will get more and more nervous until Monday.

And then it will end, one way or the other.

For the first time in forever, on Monday morning I don't walk Tara and Sebastian.

I just let them out in the backyard to do their business. Tara is clearly not happy about it; she stares at me with a combination of confusion and disdain.

Ricky spent the night at Will Rubenstein's, so Laurie and I have breakfast at six o'clock. I can barely eat anything, which is just as well, because I am so nervous that I would just throw it up.

I drive to the office for my seven o'clock meeting with Eddie Dowd. He is not going to be there; we've both known that since we set it up.

I park where I always do, in an outdoor lot just down the street. I have a yearly spot there, although I don't get much use out of it. The upside is I don't have to worry about feeding money into the meters on the street.

I try to act casual as I walk, but inside I feel so tense that if someone stuck a pin in me, I would fly around erratically, like a balloon with the air escaping. I am scared to death and dreading what is going to happen, but I'm just as scared that it won't.

As I reach the door that leads up to my office, I hear a shout and then a gunshot. I tense even more, but after a beat I realize the bullet did not hit me.

That is always a plus.

I turn and it seems like people are running everywhere, but in actuality they're just coming from different angles to the same spot. There is Laurie, and Corey, and Marcus, and Willie, and Pete Stanton, and a boatload of cops, all in plain clothes.

I run toward the same place where they are gathering, though I truly doubt that my legs are strong enough to get me there. They feel like they are made of cotton.

When I get there, a figure is supine on the ground. He's been shot in the right shoulder and is bleeding, but he's conscious. He looks up at me but does not say anything.

An officer is attending to him; I'm sure the EMTs will be here momentarily. His gun is on the ground next to him.

I turn to Pete Stanton. "You waited until he got his gun out?"

He nods. "Right. Needed to get him in the act. That way no asshole defense lawyer like you can get him off."

"He could have gotten a shot off . . . at me."

Pete shrugs. "These are the chances we have to take in the police biz."

I don't want to insult him any more because I need him. "You coming with me to court?"

He nods. "Let's go."

Before we do, I take one more look at the wounded man lying on the ground.

Chuck Holmes.

Formerly known as Richie Sanford.

Brother of Julie.

He's no longer off the grid.

Your Honor, the defense is requesting that you re-open testimony."

We are meeting in the judge's chambers at my request. Present are Judge Baron, Godfrey, Pete Stanton, and me. I would have liked to delay the meeting until my legs stopped shaking, but by that time Tony would be up for parole.

"On what grounds?" the judge asks.

"There has been an incident this morning. Police shot a man who was attempting to kill me. This man is the real murderer of Frankie Zimmer and Raymond Hackett, in addition to many others. Captain Stanton is prepared to testify to all of this."

Judge Baron turns to Pete. "Captain Stanton?"

"I agree with every word of that."

The Judge turns to Godfrey, who puts up a mild resistance, while knowing that it is futile. Pete has an excellent reputation, and what he has said has to carry significant weight with the judge.

It is basically a no-brainer for Judge Baron. For him to refuse would be to raise the possibility of thwarting justice, and certainly opening up the entire case to an obvious appeal. To go along with it merely means delaying the charge to the jury by a few hours.

"Very well," Judge Baron says. "Captain Stanton can testify and then be subject to cross-examination. Then you can both give another brief closing argument, emphasis on *brief*. Those arguments shall be limited to the new evidence that is going to be before the jury." Then, "Let's go."

We head into the courtroom, and the jury is brought in. I don't have time to tell Tony what is going on; he's going to be in for quite a surprise.

Judge Baron tells the jury that they will be hearing some additional testimony, and that even though this may seem unusual, they should give it no more or less weight than any previous testimony.

I call Pete to the stand, and I start with a history lesson. I let him take the jury through the incident that resulted in the death of Julie Sanford. That includes the attempted collection on Josh Winkler, the resulting gunfire, and the stray bullet from the gun of TJ Richardson that hit and killed Julie.

I also have him discuss what the jury has heard before, that four members of the Fulton Street Boyz got their assignments direct from the Blood Dragons: Richardson, Zimmer, Hackett, and Tony Birch. They were a gang within a gang.

Pete says that the conduit between the Blood Dragons and the four men was Russell Estrada, but that the orders always came from Luther. None of this was anything Pete was involved with, but I had asked him to study the case files over the weekend, and he has done so.

"Did Julie Sanford have a brother?" I ask.

Pete nods. "Yes. His name was Richie; he was twelve years older than his sister. The family was obviously decimated by the loss of Julie, and Richie left home in the months after the incident. He fell off the grid; there was no known trace of him in the years since."

I introduce as evidence an affidavit from Donna Sanford, Julie's sister, confirming everything that Pete is saying. Laurie had gotten it from her over the weekend. I say that Donna is available to testify if the judge finds it necessary; what I don't say is that she might be reluctant now, given that her missing brother has just been shot.

"Can you describe the events of this weekend?" I ask, leaving it open-ended. Pete is an experienced witness and knows what is required; I trust him to take it and run with it.

"You told me that you discovered that there was a bug planted in your office. You said you suspected that Chuck Holmes, the man who worked for Mr. Birch, had planted it when he visited a few weeks ago.

"You then deliberately made statements while you were in the office indicating that you had another suspect that you were going to reveal before the court. It was a rival gang leader to the Blood Dragons, though the person you spoke about was totally fictitious. You also said that you had negative information about Julie Sanford's father, that he had been involved in the drug trade. You were also going to reveal that to the court. That was also fictitious."

"Did I say in these discussions that I was confident it would result in Mr. Birch being acquitted?"

"Yes. You were speaking for the benefit of the person who planted the bug, hoping that it would goad him into action."

"What happened this morning?"

"You went to your office at seven A.M., as you had planned and spoken about in your office over the weekend. I and other officers were positioned in place, surveilling the entire area.

"As you suspected, the suspect appeared and drew his gun, apparently intent on shooting you in the back as you were entering your office. We yelled for him to freeze, but he continued in the act, so he was shot and wounded by police fire before he could get a shot off."

"Captain Stanton, was Mr. Holmes concealing his real identity?"

"Yes. He was Richard Sanford, the brother of Julie Sanford."

I introduce a photograph of Richie Sanford, which Laurie had gotten from Donna when they met this weekend. There is no question that it is a photograph of the man we had known as Chuck Holmes.

I turn Pete over to Godfrey and go back to the defense table. Tony's mouth is still open in amazement. "Holy shit," he says.

"You got that right."

Godfrey is not about to go down without a fight, and I don't blame him. The unfortunate truth is that his case is still winnable.

"Captain Stanton, do you have any evidence whatsoever

that Mr. Holmes, or Mr. Sanford, killed Frankie Zimmer?"

"I do not."

"Do you have any evidence whatsoever that Mr. Holmes, or Mr. Sanford, killed Raymond Hackett?"

"I do not."

"Does the fact that Mr. Holmes, or Mr. Sanford, drew a gun in an apparent attempt on Mr. Carpenter's life implicate him in those other deaths?"

"Not directly."

"Based on what you know at this moment, will you be arresting him for the murder of Mr. Zimmer or Mr. Hackett?"

"Not yet, but we will be investigating like hell." Way to go, Pete.

"Mr. Holmes, or Mr. Sanford, worked with Mr. Birch. Is it possible that they were on the same side, perhaps coconspirators?"

"I have no evidence of that, nor do I know why a coconspirator with Mr. Birch would be trying to kill Mr. Birch's lawyer."

"Yet," Godfrey says, ignoring the last part of what Pete said. "You have no evidence *yet*. No further questions."

Godfrey's second closing argument mirrors his cross-examination of Pete.

In his view we have no idea why Chuck Holmes tried to kill me, or whether he was a coconspirator with Tony. But the facts are what they are, and they all point to Tony's guilt in the murder of Zimmer and Hackett.

In Godfrey's telling, there's nothing new here, it's just another attempt to distract and divert. The jury has heard the facts during the full length of this trial, and that is what they should focus on.

It's not a bad argument . . . not bad at all.

"Mr. Godfrey would have you believe that nothing has changed," I say when it's my turn. "He is like the Wizard of Oz saying, 'Pay no attention to the man behind the curtain.' But it is your job to pay attention, and please allow me to explain how in fact everything has changed.

"Throughout this trial I've tried to demonstrate how all the clues pointing to Mr. Birch's guilt were too obvious, too easy. For him to have left those clues would have been either monumentally stupid, or deliberately self-destructive. But I didn't tell you another explanation, because the truth is that I did not have one. Well, now I do.

"Every single act can be explained through the prism of Richie Sanford's guilt. Mr. Birch believed that he had been summoned to a meeting with Mr. Zimmer at the bar that night. He had received a call on his cell phone. Who knew Mr. Birch's cell phone number? Richie Sanford. It would have been easy to disguise his voice, and Mr. Birch had not spoken to Mr. Zimmer in years.

"Who could have committed the murders precisely at times when Mr. Birch happened not to have an alibi? Mr. Sanford. He had access to Mr. Birch's calendar.

"Who could have buried the gun in Mr. Birch's yard? Mr. Sanford. He certainly knew where his employer lived.

"Who could have placed the handkerchief with the DNA on it, along with the gun? Mr. Sanford. He would have had easy access to one of Mr. Birch's handkerchiefs. And if you remember, there was trace DNA from a second person on that handkerchief. We won't have the test results for a while, and you won't have them during your deliberations. But are you sure it won't turn out to be Mr. Sanford's DNA?

"What about motive? Mr. Sanford's life was upended by the tragic killing of his sister. The man who did it died in prison. So Mr. Sanford, tormented by the memory, donned a fake identity and went to work for Mr. Birch. During the murder trial back then, it came out that Mr. Birch, along with Mr. Hackett and Mr. Zimmer, were part of that gang group of four.

"So Mr. Sanford set out to kill them or destroy all of their lives. And then when he found out about Russell

Estrada, and Josh Winkler, and Luther, he killed them as well. He killed everyone who was involved in that awful day when his sister died. I am horrified to say that I believe he got some of that information from the listening device he placed in my office.

"And then he tried to kill me. Why? Because he was afraid I was going to use some new evidence to prevent Mr. Birch from spending a life behind bars. And he thought I was going to implicate his father, who in truth had done nothing wrong. It enraged him, so he came after me, as I knew he would.

"Good police work saved me. And now you have to save Tony Birch. He does not deserve what has happened to him, any more than Richie Sanford's other victims deserved their fate.

"Thank you." I smile a fake relieved smile. "I promise this is the last closing argument you will have to hear."

I head back to the defense table with that same sickening feeling I had before.

It's out of my hands.

W hen a jury returns a quick verdict, I always assume it is bad news.

When they take a long time, I always assume it is bad news.

I am not the most rational person during a verdict watch.

This time it took a day and a half, sort of midrange. I think it's bad news.

Judge Baron comes in and we all rise. Eddie and I flank Tony. Sometimes clients ask me before the jury is about to come in how I think it's going to wind up. Tony doesn't ask; he's smart enough to know my answer won't matter in the slightest.

Willie sits behind me in the front row; Laurie is on his left and Corey is on his right. They look nervous. Join the club.

Judge Baron does not beat around the bush. As soon as the jury is seated, he sets things in motion, and within thirty seconds Tony, Eddie, and I are standing and waiting to hear the news.

I have my hand on Tony's shoulder; it's one of my superstitions.

It doesn't always work.

Another thing I always do as a verdict is about to be read is stop breathing, but that's not voluntary. There cannot be anything more intense and pressure filled than the moment a verdict is announced.

"As it relates to count one, the first-degree homicide of Franklin Zimmer, we, the jury, in the case of the *State of New Jersey versus Anthony Birch,* find the defendant, Anthony Birch, not guilty."

The air comes out of the balloon; Tony and I both sink about six inches as our legs almost give way. I barely hear the second verdict; there is no way Tony can be acquitted of killing Zimmer and not Hackett. Sure enough, the words "not guilty" pierce through the haze.

Tony and I hug; these are pretty much the only man hugs I can tolerate. Then he hugs Eddie; Eddie has done a great job and is welcome on our team anytime; he's a permanent member of the starting lineup.

I turn and hug Laurie, which is even better than hugging Tony. Then Judge Baron gavels the hugging to a stop. He thanks the jury for their service and tells Tony he's free to go.

Tony goes off to sign some papers, and Godfrey comes over with a congratulatory handshake. It's a bit perfunctory and half-hearted, but he fought long and hard and then lost, so I get where he's coming from.

We all wait for Tony to finish the paperwork, and then we walk through the now-empty gallery area to the exit.

When we get outside, we see Sondra at the bottom of the steps, with Zoey on a leash.

More significant, Zoey sees Tony. I don't know how many steps she takes with each lunge, it's more like she just flies over them. She lands on Tony and they go tumbling to the ground, him laughing, or crying, I can't tell which. Her tail is wagging and her tongue is licking; suddenly she is the happiest dog I have ever seen.

I have been around a lot of reunions, but this one is my all-time favorite.

We used to hold our victory parties at Charlie's, but not anymore.

In those days they were composed primarily of humans, but now we've added dogs and kids to the mix. So we have them, like we're having this one, at the Tara Foundation.

The humans present, in addition to me and Laurie, are Ricky, Tony, Sam, Willie, Sondra, Marcus, Corey, Edna, Eddie, Pete Stanton, and Vince Sanders. Pete and Vince are here because the food is free, and because we're having it early, before the evening's basketball games begin.

On the canine side, we have Tara, Sebastian, Simon Garfunkel, Zoey, and Willie and Sondra's two dogs, Cash and Aggie. Then, just to make things more chaotic and fun, Willie lets the twenty-five dogs we have up for adoption join the fun.

Charlie's has catered the human food and drink; PetSmart has handled the kibble and biscuits. Laurie has made some eggnog, just to add the endless-Christmas touch.

Vince is completely in character when he comes over and says, "No nachos?" He looks amazed. "Who throws a party and doesn't serve nachos?"

"Sorry, Vince, my fault. I should have checked with you. You're one of the heroes of this case."

"How's that?"

"When you were stuffing your face and insulting me at Charlie's the other night, you said that dead bodies kept following me, like it was my fault."

"So?"

"So you were right; it made me realize that somebody was monitoring my movements and what I was saying. It broke the case."

"I'm a goddamn hero. A hero without nachos."

Vince goes off to suffer through some burgers and fries. I walk over to Tony. I did not have a chance to talk that much with Tony after the trial, so he has some questions. "So Chuck . . . I mean Sanford . . . was putting on an act? That whole 'Mr. Tony' thing?"

I nod. "He had me fooled."

"Until he didn't. But why did he set me up and then kill Estrada and Luther and the others after I was in jail?"

"I'm not sure, but I think he only learned about those guys, and Winkler, from listening in on me in the office. When he heard that they were involved in the incident that killed his sister, they got added to the hit list."

"What made you suspect him?"

"Like I said in court, he had access to everything, and he was in my office, so he could have planted the bug then. But it was also something he said while he was testifying."

"What's that?"

"He said I told him Estrada set the fire, but I never did. He was saying it to hurt our case."

"Why did they set the fire?" Tony asks. "I had nothing that could hurt Luther or Estrada."

"Sanford must have gotten word to them that you did, maybe through an anonymous phone call. Could have been tapes, documents, whatever. They weren't taking any chances.

"It was Sanford's way of drawing them out; I'll bet he followed Estrada that day and learned where they worked out of and tracked their movements. He was thorough."

Tony shakes his head in amazement. "You are really good at this." Then, "What about Banner?"

"He was supposed to be part of the frame-up; you were going down for three murders. Chuck didn't realize that an out-of-state murder could not be part of this trial; evidence about it wasn't even admissible."

Laurie comes over, as does Corey. Laurie looks out toward the center of the huge room, where the dogs are playing and wrestling . . . Zoey in the middle of it. "I think Zoey is glad to have you back," she says.

"I'm glad to be back, and so glad to have her. And I owe it all to all of you."

"Willie made it happen," I say.

"You going to rebuild the auto shop?" Corey asks.

Tony nods. "And we're going to expand." He points to Laurie and me. "Along with my new partners."

Laurie smiles. "I think it's going to be a great investment, and maybe Andy can work down there on spark plugs and transmissions and stuff."

I shake my head. "No way. I'm a semiretired lawyer."